MORE ADVANCE PRAISE FOR *MOUTHQUAKE*:

"*Mouthquake*, the most vividly palpable Montreal novel in English since Mordecai Richler, puts the legend back in urban and the realism back in magic. Part queer amour fou and part personal demon-wrestling, this tall tale evokes like none other the delirious world of childhood subjectivity, *Alice in Wonderland* meets *The Tin Drum* meets *The 400 Blows*. Tectonically written, from pavement abjection and hallucinogenic dream life to the intensely lived-in body and space of an unforgettable narrator, *Mouthquake* demands to be read under sturdy furniture or on an open park bench."

—**Thomas Waugh**, AUTHOR OF
The Fruit Machine: Twenty Years of Writings on Queer Cinema

"Daniel Allen Cox is a maestro of form-querying-queer. You think you have his number, you think he's in the bed beside you, but he's up, off, boldly probing. Our pleasure as readers is to keep pace with his intriguing corpus. In *Mouthquake*, Daniel mouths the music of memory as he dials us into the minutiae of stuttering."

—**Anakana Schofield**, AUTHOR OF *Malarky* AND *Martin John*

"In *Mouthquake*, Daniel Allen Cox ventures into the lions' den of language and unleashes his extraordinary stutter. The result, a shimmering, always surprising frottage of Montreal, has the queer wit of a Britten aria."

—**John Greyson**, DIRECTOR OF *Zero Patience* AND *Lilies*

mouthquake

a novel

DANIEL ALLEN COX

arsenal pulp press · vancouver

ARSENAL PULP PRESS
Suite 202–211 East Georgia St.
Vancouver, BC V6A 1Z6 Canada
arsenalpulp.com

The publisher gratefully acknowledges the support of the Canada Council for the Arts and the British Columbia Arts Council for its publishing program, and the Government of Canada (through the Canada Book Fund) and the Government of British Columbia (through the Book Publishing Tax Credit Program) for its publishing activities.

Canada

This is a work of fiction. Any resemblance of characters to persons either living or deceased is purely coincidental.

Part of the chapter "Coprofagia" was published, in a different form, in *Crooked Fagazine*, Issue 2, 2013.

The creation of this work was made possible by the financial support of the Conseil des arts et des lettres du Québec.

**Conseil des arts
et des lettres**
Québec

Design and cover photograph by Gerilee McBride
Edited by Susan Safyan

Printed and bound in Canada

Library and Archives Canada Cataloguing in Publication

Cox, Daniel Allen, author
Mouthquake : a novel / Daniel Allen Cox.

Issued in print and electronic formats.
ISBN 978-1-55152-604-1 (paperback).—ISBN 978-1-55152-605-8 (epub)

I. Title.

PS8605.O934M69 2015   C813'.6   C2015-903344-6
                                                C2015-903345-4

I am delighted to add another unplayable work to the repertoire.

—*Arnold Schoenberg*

ANTONIO

UNCERTAIN MUSIC

I've come to realize that if anything happened, there was probably music.

Now I lean in close to listen.

It has come back to me in variations, in music I don't recognize. Memory can defragment, but it never resembles the original experience.

The image itself is fairly uncertain. I'm small and standing in front of a record player. The receiver is silver and covered with dials. There are tiny tuning meters in little glass windows filled with yellow light, stacked like apartments in a building. The needles wobble back and forth, showing the science of the music. In this image, I'm not sure what the song is. I'm staring at the record spinning on the turntable. The label hypnotizes me, creating a swirl of colour in my head that didn't exist before. The grooves orbit past me like black oil, smooth and perfect. I'm just discovering my relationship to the substance of vinyl. This record doesn't have any scratches. The arm bobs as the record turns. There's a slight warp. I want to see the needle up close so I pretend I'm tiny and jump onto the turntable in my mind. You might say I haven't come back since.

As soon as I land beside the arm and admire the boy-sized diamond tip at my feet, I begin to feel I'm not alone. There's a presence behind me. Don't ask me what the clues are: shadow, body heat, breath on the back of my downy neck. For whatever reason, I don't want to turn around. Maybe it's because I know the music will stop.

That's all I have at the moment.

Now, certain music gives me certain feelings.

Uncertain music gives me uncertain feelings.

When I speak, it comes out like a weird kind of song-making.

I don't always understand myself, the same way I don't always understand lyrics.

This is where we stand for now. I wonder what this all means. In the meantime, I open my mouth. Play every song I can find, full volume, and backward. Pronounce every word, no matter how it comes out.

I listen and try to remember.

I speak.

IMAGINARY FRIENDS

The 1970s were all about strange men talking to little kids on the street. These were adults that none of the other adults saw. Our imaginary friends, if you will.

Take *Sesame Street*. For years, nobody believed Big Bird that Mr. Snuffleupagus was real, that a woolly mammoth lived just up the block. He was never there when they went to find him. I somehow feel that even if they had looked right at Snuffy, he'd be invisible to them. Amazing how their minds were closed, especially back when everybody smoked pot. In a closed mind, a notion is extinct before the evidence can be presented. There's an inner eyelid that our tear ducts always forget to lubricate.

I never saw it as a kid, but there's a *Sesame Street* episode in which an adult finally believes in Snuffy. The first person who ever told Big Bird that they believed was Buffy Sainte-Marie. She didn't have to see the mammoth to know his trueness. She said so in a song, and it changed everything. It broke the hardness in Big Bird's young heart. When an animal that big and that yellow gains hope, it becomes bright and powerful. Blinding to the spirit.

Sometimes it takes music to make something real. Sometimes you have to sing it out in a song.

But was Buffy real? She and Big Bird both had feathers.

As a boy, I didn't know whether or not I believed in the existence of woolly mammoths. On TV they looked too exaggerated and fake—lips too human and eyes too big. In colouring books, the lines were always drawn too sharply. The mammoths were placed in impossible situations, fraternizing with animals they'd never encounter in the wild. For years I assumed that Big Bird was making it all up.

I suppose my perspective started to change the day we went to the *Musée des beaux-arts.* The museum was hosting a travelling Smithsonian exhibit that featured a woolly mammoth skeleton, complete with tusks. Extinct and chilled, it had an extreme case of freezer burn.

My mom tried to get me to say "mammoth," but it came out "Chiquitita." I was a strange boy.

I was less of a boy, however, and more of a German Shepherd. I'd always had a keener sense of hearing than is appropriate for a human. I'd always been more interested in the sounds toys make than in the toys themselves: The click of unlocking the docking port on the Death Star. Drooling wet swish of rolling marbles in my mouth. Clatter of plastic bowling pins scattering hollow down the hallway. Rain of random Lego spilling on the floor. Tiny metallic thunder of toy cars reaming each other in smash-up derby. The snap and fart of blowing bubbles into toxic green goop. The ping of an Easy-Bake Oven when the cake was done. Soft thud of Nerf balls pounding dents into delicate tufts of cat fur. Satanic growl of a talking Teddy Ruxpin running low on batteries. Heart-breaking plastic crunch when an adult stepped on a toy and destroyed it.

My ears were permanently pricked.

Another indication was the affinity I felt for the main character on the TV show *The Littlest Hobo*, the German Shepherd who rescued people. My favourite episode was the one where the lost boy was trapped in a meat fridge. The dog found him and alerted the adults with a series of intelligent barks. He wasn't even thinking of all that meat, just the boy. How unselfish. Of course, the boy was a kind of meat, but still.

I cried at the end of every show because when the grownups went to thank the dog, he was always gone. He would walk down the road into the sunset, then turn around once, with his tongue hanging out. Was that a goodbye? Where was he going? Why didn't he stay if he liked the people he saved? If he had a home somewhere, why did he always leave it? Why didn't he have a name? I cried and cried during the credits. For me, sadness was confusion. It was a scrunched-up face that got red and hot, a runny nose that spilled into my mouth, and not being able to catch my breath. Forever panting in front of the TV.

The truth is that the Littlest Hobo was called away. I could hear a dog whistle being blown just off-screen. It made me turn and look. I was old enough to know that the Littlest Hobo had a life outside the TV. The best way to find him was for him to find me. I had to get lost and in trouble somehow. Couldn't be too hard. If I wasn't going out to buy Rothmans King Size cigarettes for the neighbour, then I usually didn't know where I was going, so it was perfect. I put on my boots, coat, and hat, but couldn't find my mitts so I wore another pair of boots on my hands. I turned the door knob with the heels, and left the apartment for nowhere in particular.

Montreal was a nonstop blizzard. Hockey fans couldn't get to the Forum in time for the puck to drop. Babies couldn't get through the snow on the highways so they were born in ambulances and taxis. This was decades before the mega-city merger, so determining the town of birth was kind of a toss-up. Drivers guesstimated where they were, because they couldn't see through the blinding white. Parking meters were lost under drifts and became snow people, so parking was free if you could get anywhere close to the curb. But no one could. Snow got in our boots because boots weren't high enough. Toe bones hardened into icicles. Snow rose up the windows so high that the horizon was over my head. And it was only January.

I tried to take a bus, but the driver wouldn't pick up a kid with four feet. He totally misread my species. I slinked through the alleys peeking through half-open doors into restaurant kitchens, waiting until the cooks cleared off so I could run in and steal a meatball or two, or a plate of fries, careful to avoid taking any vegetables by mistake. I was good at dodging kicks from the staff. But those restaurant back doors mostly turned out to be mirages. I was cold and hungry, staring into fantasies in the cinder block.

Still no celebrity CBC dog.

I was lost for sure. It was where I wanted to be ... but now what? My face was freezing off, nose starting to hurt. I had fallen so many times on my booted hands that I just started to walk on all fours. The sound of a Snoopy Sno Cone machine crushing ice. I was famished, so I scoured my pockets and picked through the fur under my toque. Not a scrap. I stuck my schnoz through holes in garbage bags. Other animals had been there before me. My sniffer got happy because I found pizza crusts—tomato-flavoured popsicles—my favourites.

The more I wondered where the Littlest Hobo was, the more I wondered if I had become him.

It got dark really fast. The street lights gave everything long and jagged shadows. So many weird shapes on the snow in front of me. There was one that grew and grew even when I stayed still. Waiting to cross the light to wade through the snow, I encountered a species unknown to me. A monster. He must have weighed more than 500 pounds. He had long silver and brown dreads twisted like industrial cable and frayed at the ends like a stiff boot brush. He wore giant boots of floppy black leather, and a thick miasma of garlic hung around him, bad breath swirling in a cloud. The lines of his face were contoured with the soot of bus exhaust, and his nose mushroomed blackheads and collected runnels of oil. Heavy iron-link chains swung from his neck. He moved with the grace of a snow bank.

This creature said something to me. It came out of his mouth not as words, but as snowflake shapes. I nodded to the shapes, and we had an understanding, there on the corner in the thick of winter. He laid a hand on my head, which made me still. When he patted my toque, it felt like I was being bashed by a warm, raw steak. When he laughed, it sounded like the engine of a bus in trouble.

I may have been mistaken about his laugh; there actually was a bus revving its engine uselessly, wheels spinning because it couldn't cross the intersection for all the snow. It was full of passengers. The mammoth lumbered to the front of the bus and attached one of his chains to the front bumper. He leaned forward, strained against the chain, and started to pull. The wheels didn't turn. They slid. The passengers cheered through the foggy windows.

I had just seen my first live woolly mammoth.

It has been years since the winter has given us such snow.

I still watch *Sesame Street* faithfully to this day. It's not that painful to be a believer.

Now, enough time has passed for me to understand what happened that day: It was my knighthood as a weirdo. I felt a strange energy pass from his hand through the top of my skull, the energy of outsiders and the misunderstood or the not-understood-enough, those who do not apologize for their strange behaviour. I've felt the weight of his hand ever since. The sound of the rattling chains follow me everywhere and interfere with the signals I have to intercept as part of daily life. He was my first imaginary friend, but not my last.

I've since learned that if you have more than one imaginary friend, there's no guarantee they'll speak to each other.

CHAMPION DES CHAMPIONS

Back then, when winter thawed in Quebec, it came as the end of an environmental siege. The weather usually held us captive for more than six months at a time, locked inside our dry, over-heated apartments dreaming of the day we would see vegetation again, even a single blade of grass, or be able to cross the street without getting killed by a snow plough. There were several fake thaws we didn't trust. False starts. But once spring came for real, it was a violent beauty. Avalanches of ice fell off roofs and crashed onto sidewalks. Icicles rained like spears. Lakes formed in intersections, forcing cars to drive around ice floes and other debris. The snow melted to reveal the hideous wreckage of lost and abandoned bicycles that had become mere piles of rust, battered by the sidewalk ploughs. We were happy not to be casualties of the season like that.

The Grand Antonio and I didn't speak, but we understood each other nonetheless. The world around us overvalued speech. They were putting their energy into all the wrong things.

He'd belly laugh whenever he saw me. It sounded like a cement truck rumbling down the street. I'd crawl onto the tiny space beside him on the sidewalk bench, the small corner not occupied by his fat. I had to puff myself out not to get crushed—it was a really tight squeeze. One of his braids always landed in my lap. Before we'd start the day's business, I had to pluck the clover and beetles out of his hair, leftovers from whatever park he had slept in the night before. I had to untangle caterpillars from the wires that knotted his braids, and pick out ants that had gotten crushed in the beeswax that he used to keep them together. We had a symbiotic relationship that way. I was an obedient dog.

I always wondered where he slept, but it remained a mystery to me. He just kind of wandered off at the end of the day. Couldn't have been the mountain because it was too far and too high, given his weight. Parc Père Marquette was likelier. But wasn't any park too cold in the winter? I have a hard time picturing him cooped up in a Montreal apartment, boxed in between neighbours, confined to a living room barely twice his size (sitting on a couch and doing what?), a kitchen with a mouse's refrigerator and a thimbleful of dinner, a bathroom the size of one of his legs.

I didn't know much about the history of my position except that the previous employee was another dog. I got the feeling that it had died. Dogs died all the time in the '70s. The summers were too hot. I never asked about it, because I could see the pain in his face whenever a dog came by, sniffing. He often gave our dinner to strays. Made me so jealous!

My primary job was to bring people to the bench, to find suckers we could sell to. I knew instinctively what to do. Sometimes I pretended to fall on the sidewalk and skin my knee, and someone would inevitably pick me up and sit me on the bench. Then they belonged to Antonio. My favourite scam was to crawl between a gentleman's legs when he was distracted, say, waiting for the bus and reading the *Montreal Star*. I'd tie his shoelaces together and he'd fall into Antonio's lap, where the selling would begin. Antonio would reach into the garbage bag beside him and pull out a postcard at random. The postcards were bricolage curiosities he made himself, warped with LePage's wood glue not fully dried, old photos of him in his fat youth, twenty years prior, posing with the famous and influential, defaced by inscriptions in block letters and black ink declaring his greatness. How someone with sausage fingers could create such elaborate and delicate bas-relief is just another mystery I'll add to the heap.

These folios told the story of his life, of how he became "World Champion Number One," as he put it. So it's understandable that he got upset when business was less than spectacular. Antonio showed all of his emotions at once. He was a constantly changing storm of happiness and rage and sadness and confusion.

Ten dollars.

I'll give you a dollar.

One dollar? Are you c-c-c-c-crazy? This is Harvey Keitel, my friend. Do you like movies? Movies make me sad. Nobody is alive anymore still. They dance and they play with each other and sometimes sing. Sing, yes. But nobody is alive. Anymore still. Anyways. Sorry.

Okay, five dollars.

You come here to my bench to insult me and the dog!

I don't see a dog.

See what you want to see. Ha. Number-One world champion wrestler stands in front of you and you see ... Ah, maybe you think I am the opera singer too cheap to sing? Here, I will sing for you. Lucky for you, today I ate the singing garlic. Today we are Italian. You also, *bambino.*

Fine, I'll give you the ten dollars.

What, ten? Now is fifteen. You talk too much.

Just give me the damn postcard.

Seventy-five! Woof woof woof woof woof woof woof woof! *Volare, oh, oh, Cantare, ohohoho.*

Amazing how much money we made, given that most customers ran away once he started barking Dean Martin lyrics.

The priceless ten-dollar collection contained, in various layers at the bottom of the garbage bag: the Grand Antonio posing with the Dean himself, Rowan Atkinson, Jack Welch, Ed Sullivan, Liza Minnelli, Leo Sayer, Wilt Chamberlain, Scatman John, Carly Simon, Anthony Quinn, Johnny Carson, Pavarotti, Liberace. Countless others. It's said that his garbage bag was the single most detailed record of celebrity socialite life in Montreal in the 1970s and 1980s. Antonio's heaps of scrap paper were often the only proof that something had ever happened.

There was one postcard, I later discovered, that he never offered for sale. It was a photo-transfer of him at Birks jewellery store, looping a diamond pendant over the neck of Marilyn Monroe, past the golden curls and onto the milky skin of her neck, while she threw her head back and laughed, and a police officer fainted just behind her into the waiting arms of a priest.

There is no record of Marilyn Monroe, the hottest stutterer to sex the world, ever having visited Montreal. But there was a postcard.

Sometimes people asked Antonio questions they shouldn't have, questions he didn't like to answer. Sometimes they asked about me. We told them ridiculous stories, said that a construction company had sold me for a pair of nosebleed tickets at the Forum. The best way not to answer a question was to answer it wrongly. You had to say something.

He kept his money in different places. A stack in the bottom of each shoe that got so compressed that fives turned into hundreds. He had a hollowed-out loaf of crusty Italian bread in which he kept our coins. He made me lift the little cannonball once a day so I would grow strong and big like he was. I was in charge of the one-dollar bills. I kept them in my pants where no one would get them.

Our food situation was quite simple. Passersby opened their grocery bags to Antonio, in deference to his status as local royalty. He just reached his prosciutto-sized fist into someone's brown paper Steinberg's bag and pulled out, say, a jar of mayonnaise. Out of the next bag came a loaf of white bread. A third bag gave up salami and pickles. It was like watching a magic show. People lined up to open their bags for the privilege of making this fat man fatter.

Of course I ate the spoils. It was a dog's paradise.

I must admit that, for most of that summer, with Antonio communicating to me in gestures, grunts, and bellows but otherwise wordlessly, I grew unsatisfied. At some point I craved to be spoken to, as any good sidekick ankle-biter does. There was a distinct absence of commands, barked and followed, in which I could anchor myself in relation to him, a tiny satellite of a huge planet, uncertain of my place. I longed to be praised, disciplined, touched, held, and taught. I needed to find an orbit.

I think Antonio eventually figured that out. Perhaps he had a frightful vision of losing another small creature to the streets. The thing with runaways is they never give you advance notice before they take off. And he was becoming attached to me. I noticed that every time I met him on the bench, he gave me a little more room, squeezing his heft impossibly into the opposite corner, as uncomfortable as that must've been for him.

One day, he took me to an Expos baseball game. I had never been to *le Stade olympique* before, but I knew all about it. I had wanted to see Michael Jackson when he came, but my mom told me he wasn't for kids.

I hoped this would be the day Antonio spoke to me.

Just a few years after the 1976 Olympics, the city was still brand-new at being famous, and still waking up to sticky, wet dreams in the morning. The dew of dawn and promise, a planet envious, nothing like it to make people fuck and have kids; let's make it bigger, this ripple of hope and promise and newness, let's build weird buildings and tell people this is how the future will look. We will agree to be prematurely futuristic for the money, the tourists, and the fame. That is when the story was good. When it was all genius architecture by genius architects, geometry and concrete, tunnels and electricity, when it was fantasy islands in the river, a mountain peak kissed by fate. We will agree to forget the past. We will agree to ignore the inevitability of decline. We will agree to smile at each other, although we don't feel like it.

But even as a puppy, I could see it all falling apart.

Antonio made sure we covered as much of the city terrain as we could. Given his size, that wasn't hard to do. We rode the Papineau and Sherbrooke buses for free and sat where we wanted. I yelled at people when I saw them hold their noses. How dare they! I guess I got used to his smell. When we got off the bus, I rode on Antonio's shoulders as he walked toward the stadium. I was perched several feet above a sea of people, my feet entwined in the chains around his neck. My personal mammoth. Antonio cheered all the way there, growling greetings to his admirers. But we didn't go to the wickets with everybody else. Antonio made a detour past a construction site, another patch of corruption, perpetually unfinished, this Montreal of mine. There was a rumour that every day, truckloads of cement were being diverted elsewhere—that's why the stadium was taking forever to finish. Once inside, he grabbed about sixteen hotdogs for free from a concession stand, and we headed into the stadium right in time for the national anthem. I found a free seat, but Antonio stood. He wouldn't have fit.

When the anthem was sung, he chimed in with another Dean Martin aria:

When the moon eats your eye like a big pizza pie, that's amore…

People came up to ask for autographs, but I think some of them mistook him for Youppi!, the shaggy orange Expos mascot.

The 'Spos were playing the Phillies. Carter hit a double his first time up, then a home run. Raines singled a rocket to centre and stole second. Cromartie with something called a sacrifice fly and the Rock took third. Double, rocket, sacrifice fly. These words came out of a transistor radio that an old man beside me was holding, but I didn't know what they meant. *Nos Amours* ran around in their red, white, and baby-blue pyjamas. The Kid came out of the dugout to fist-pump and get the crowd riled up, which they responded to in the strangest way. The seats of the stadium were the kind that clacked when you pushed them down into sitting position. Hard plastic against metal, far louder than a clap. But when everyone stood up, it didn't sound like clacks. Instead, the noise collected like atomic particles into a roar that shook the entire building. Antonio just stood there and absorbed the shaking. He was trying to feel it. Maybe he was testing himself to see if he was earthquake proof for some future unknown trial. I watched him with admiration. We rode the quake together.

Antonio could see that I was confused by the finer points of the game. He finally spoke to me during the seventh-inning stretch, looking right through me with his aquarium orbs, capillaries swimming in a decilitre of happy tears:

The shortstop, he looks crazy. You see him?

No, which one is he?

There, one between he is. You see now? You watch, people think he doesn't know where he goes anymore, still. But he knows exactly. To be number-one *champion mondiale*, you must be a good actor. Go any direction at the same time. It's science, wrestling, baseball.

Science, wrestling, baseball?

No, it's prosciutto, *b-b-b-b-bravado*.

Yes?

Yes and no. Hair also. Good, strong shortstop hair. Like yours.

Shortstop is French for *arrêt-court. Arrêt-court.*

He petted my head to make sure the information sank in, almost as if he knew that prosciutto, bravado, and hair were more memorable than foul balls, tags, check swings, and strike zones, and would ultimately be more useful to me in life.

Why do you talk like that?

Like what, how like?

Sometimes you have trouble.

Let me ask instead, rather. What is the trouble in your ears?

We were up by a run in the top of the ninth with two out. Rogers was throwing with a little extra mustard, and maybe even more *choucroute* than usual. They really wanted this one. The fans had started to throw plastic beer cups onto the field as part of the pre-celebration mayhem. The umps had to stop play several times to clean up. The Phillies' Mike Schmidt stepped up to the plate. He was the potential third out, but *le Stade* wanted more: They wanted his body to hang from the stadium rim where he could bleed out properly.

Rogers delivered a sinking fastball and Schmidt connected, sending it on a long arc into the outfield. The Hawk lunged just shy of the ball and missed it. Then he picked it up and dropped it. The crowd fell into disbelief and missed heartbeats, an audible choke. Schmidt was rounding second. Was he going for home plate? The Hawk recovered the ball and threw his arm off. We all watched his arm bounce at the edge of the infield, then once near the mound.

The catcher Gary Carter received three things at the same time: Mike Schmidt, The Hawk's arm, and the ball. He did what he could.

The ump called it.

Mike Schmidt was the third out and dead meat.

Nobody could hear what happened next.

We left through the same back door we came through.

I was convinced that Antonio knew where all the missing cement had gone. Maybe he was hoarding it. It was certainly enough to build our own city with. The time would come. He would wander right to it, and I'd either be on his shoulders or sneaking behind, a mutt between mammoth legs. Maybe there would be sixty-four Miron cement trucks lined up prettily in rows of eight, drums turning in concert, revving their Freightliner engines and shifting into tenth gear to prepare for take-off, or maybe it would be an empty Pepsi can filled with a few glops of concrete and soggy MarkTen butts rising to the top. Maybe we didn't need much. In any case, we'd have all the contraband concrete that two sidewalk Mafiosos could dream of; then they could tear this all down, the whole damn city, who cares, because we could remake it exactly how we wanted and needed to.

A QUEEREST ABDICATION

Open Letter to the People of the City of Montreal
le 26 mai 1979

I regret to announce that I have to cancel my upcoming engagement at the Montreal Forum. Actually, let me be pristinely clear about this: I don't regret the cancellation at all. You had it coming.

The Show Must Go On, but only when there is an inkling of love.

For years I was your queen. You knew it, I knew it. We were a nonstop champagne party, baby. Montreal became my Munich, and that's saying a lot. We had a proper relationship right from the very first limousine. The streets of Dorval were lined with flowers. I'll never forget how you threw them on the car and the driver had to turn on the wipers just to see through the daffodils. When you gave me a hockey jersey with the number 69 on it, I knew we had officially commenced a mutual rimming and fallen in love.

Bismillah, bismillah

I didn't take your gifts for granted. I learned French and separatism. (I'm an anti-monarchist unless the monarch is myself. My heart is split into two parts: the left is Ibiza, and the right is an independent Quebec nation.) You adopted me. Those were the good times. Because I wasn't an English Canadian, I was not the enemy and therefore, by default, a friend. When I came out onstage nearly nude except for a Beau Dommage T-shirt and you cheered, what was that for? All that love is meaningless to me now.

Scaramouche, scaramouche

When you chose someone else, don't you think you should've sent me a warning telegram via one of my stage boys, perhaps dressed in silver lamé short shorts, who would tell me, O fickle and treacherous people of Montreal, that you were planning to betray me? That you thousands, who screamed for song after song and encore after encore, bleeding me naked and dry, laryngitis be damned, had already chosen another?

When were you planning to tell me about the Prince of Papineau? The Strongman of La Petite-Patrie? The Butcher of Bonsecours? The Samson of Saint-Laurent?

And when, pray tell, O self-described Number-One fans, were you going to tell me that a 500-pound cretin who pulls buses down the street and eats fourteen chickens in a single sitting—live, dead, who knows—that this *thing* was going to make me his next meal? That you preferred the fallacy of wrestling, the crass, lowest common denominator physical entertainment, to the artistry of rock opera?

That you chose a beast over the very reincarnation of Maria Callas?

That you had come to see me destroyed?

You deserved what you got, but you never deserved me.

I learned some things about you that night, Montreal, and they are to your damnation. This is the rewriting of your history and future, and I have the lamentable pleasure of documenting it for you. I learned that you did not know how to do the fandango.

It was the night you screamed for a fourth encore. I had never done one before. The band left the stage, and I sat there at the piano in my diaper and Canadiens jersey, preparing to play a song I had written just for you. But your cheers weren't for me. They were for the monster that galumphed onstage behind me, chains hanging from his neck, slobber dripping from his face, unintelligible. He had come to get me.

That is the day you chose brute stupidity over refined genius, when 18,000 people decided to dethrone me. The cement of your city started to crumble and the rebar began to show.

That is the night the Grand Antonio—this mutant, this shameless stutterer—laced his two dreadlocked ponytails around my ankles and swung me around the stage like a carrousel while the microphone captured everything—my uncharacteristic silence, your thirst for a royal dumbing down, your hopeless return to the clutches of Commonwealth. The end of your sovereignty.

I don't suppose you care to know that under those hot lights, but hidden under his reams of fat, he tried to eat my face, and I have been under emergency beauty care ever since; a thousand young Moroccan-Dutch dancers ejaculate onto my face in regenerative and uplifting movements, the best plastic surgeons restore me to God's glory while whispering about the night Quebec died. You deserve Ottawa.

But do tell me, I'm so curious: how did you hide that wrestling ring backstage? I never saw it coming. You are dead to me, but that ring and those turnbuckles come to me in the height of nocturnal emission . . . strangely, to your credit, your aesthetics have always been impeccable. I may steal it for a show.

Montreal, now you will never hear the song that I wrote for you.

It was the greatest song that Queen never recorded.

I now formally abdicate as your leader. Go get your kicks in the lower forms of humanity, among the impaired.

Yours never more, and forget my name,

Freddie Mercury

POLAROIDED

It was only a matter of time until a kid like me was picked up by the cops.

I spent way too much time outside the house. Another problem was that I'd been acting too careful around the police. Of course it looks suspicious when you don't cross on yellow lights. It's damning when you collect chip bags and ice cream sandwich wrappers that other litterbugs leave behind. Model citizenry is usually a cover for something. I had nothing to hide, so I have no idea why I acted that way.

The officer who nabbed me was a sneaky one. He accused me of stealing the trash I was picking up, saying he'd book me if I didn't show receipts from the *dépanneur*. Naturally, I had none, so he loaded me into the front seat and drove me to the station. Where were the handcuffs? I didn't know you could ride in a police car like it was a taxi. My situation became a little clearer at the station.

I'm just going to ask you a few questions, okay?

Okay.

Do you want some juice? A glass of milk? We have donuts, too.

Sure, a donut.

Okay, then. Here you go.

D-d-d-do you have one with sprinkles? I like sprinkles a lot.

Sorry, this is all we have. Now, you know why you're here, right?

Did I do anything wrong? Am I under arrest?

So young, and you sound like a perp. No, you're not under arrest. Don't worry about that. It's come to our attention that you've been hanging around with a person of interest, a man.

Perp…What's a perp?

Funny you should ask. Nothing, it's just police language. Do you know who I'm talking about?

Um, I'm not sure.

Come on now, we've seen you with him several times. You know him. We've seen you.

Am I in trouble?

Well, no. Not if you tell us everything. And not if we believe you. So don't even try lying, because we'll know.

But what if I tell the truth and you don't believe me?

That won't happen. How did you meet this man?

Outside. I met him on the street.

Did he talk to you?

No.

Then how did you meet?

I was coming home and I wanted to cross the street but I couldn't because, um, I think, like, there were too many cars? Yeah. So he made the cars stop and let me cross. It was winter and there was a lot of snow. He had big boots that could go through it.

Were you alone?

Y-yes.

Was this in January?

Uh-huh.

Was it still light out, or was it getting dark?

Getting dark. I couldn't see him well.

You're lying.

No, I'm not!

Yes, you are. The sun doesn't set before three in the afternoon, even in January. So either you're lying about the darkness, or this bullshit little story happened later than you said it did. So which is it?

I don't remember.

Why were you alone?

I don't want to say. You're going to get the neighbour in trouble.

The neighbour won't be in trouble if you tell me the truth.

Are you a perp?

No, I'm not a perp.

I was going to get her a pack of Rothmans King Size. I always have to do that because she doesn't like to leave the house. But I don't tell my mom I do it.

That's okay.

It's okay?

Sure, no problem. At least she smokes a good brand. Wanna root beer?

Y-yy-y-yyyyyy sure!

When did you start speaking like that?

Like what?

Maybe we'll talk about that another time. Alright. Here's your root beer. Now I want you to try and remember a little better. Can you do that? Good. Did this man talk to you?

No. Is he in trouble? What did he do?

We're not sure, that's what we're trying to find out.

Did he steal something?

Yes, he steals all the time, but we already know that. We're looking at something else. Let me ask the questions, okay? What do you do when you're with him?

We just sit. On the bench.

Why?

I don't know. It's hot. People give us food. Um, they're really nice to him. Everyone, I guess, likes him. He gives the candy and cookies to me.

I see. But don't you find him gross? Doesn't he smell?

A bit. But you smell, too. All grownups do!

Huh. Now I'm going to ask you a question, and I want you to think very carefully before answering, because I don't want you to give me the wrong answer. Can you do that? Okay. Did this man ever touch you?

No.

You answered too quickly. Do you want some more time to think?

No, I don't need time to think, he didn't touch me. I want another root beer.

There is no more root beer.

I don't believe you.

Maybe there is more, but first you have to keep talking. He is a very big man. Even when you were sitting on the bench beside him, his leg never touched yours? It's a pretty small bench. There couldn't have been enough room for both of you.

Okay, maybe his leg, but it's not his fault. He's big because he's strong.

So you were lying when you said he didn't touch you.

I'm not a liar, I said!

Don't get upset, just tell me the truth. What else are you hiding? You won't get in trouble if you tell. But if you don't tell, there could be repercussions.

What are repercussions?

Bad things.

Bad things that happen to me?

Yes, possibly. That's why you have to tell me everything.

Will you tell my mom?

No. We can't tell your mom any of this.

Okay, well, I think he was standing there with chains around his neck and I was, um, like really scared. Then he put his hand on my head, because I remember it was so big it felt like I was wearing a hat. Or like someone put a baby on my head. And he laughed. I wasn't scared anymore because I could tell he was really nice.

Wait—you're saying that he touched you? With his hand?

I guess so.

Is that a yes?

Do you have any more donuts?

All kinds.

Then, yes.

That's really interesting.

Why is it interesting?

No reason. That's all we need for today. You did very, very well.

So you'll give me the root beer and donuts, and I can go?

Not just yet. I need you to come in the back with me.

Why?

We have to take your picture for the files.

But why can't we take the picture here?

The cop led me to a locker room in the back of the precinct. We were alone. Well, kind of. There was a life-sized poster of Hall & Oates in front of the lockers. They looked so real, leering at me with pretty smiles. I couldn't stop staring. The officer sat me on the wooden bench and started taking pictures of me with a Polaroid camera. The flashes flashed. What I remember most is trying to pose like Daryl Hall, with a smile as pretty. Every time he clicked, the camera spit out another grey square. He put the photos away before they developed, before I could see them.

I never saw the Grand Antonio again.

Antonio didn't do anything to me, but some people believed the cop, who just wanted an excuse to put him away. That's what some people said. He wanted to get a dirty body off his beat. There was an investigation but no trial. Kept it hush-hush and out of the press. They called in a speech therapist to ask me questions and to give expert testimony on my stutter and the events that might have triggered it. It was all about my mouth. The conversations were way over my head:

Isn't it possible that

Wouldn't you say that

Do you deny that

Is there a reasonable chance that

Can we object that

Did you feel that

Did you suspect that

Did you worry that

That that that that that that that

Did he ever

Touch kiss rub stare poke press grab show

This wasn't the language that German Shepherds used. I replied "yes" or "no" almost randomly to the questions, because I didn't understand what they were saying to me. Then I was worried I had given them all the wrong answers, the ones they would twist to get Antonio in trouble.

I would later learn that, even though their fabrications had nothing to do with the soundscape of my life, there was indeed something in my past to talk about.

I would later learn how easily the kind people of the world were destroyed.

LA GLACE

Sometimes I tell friends about my dreams. Especially if they're embarrassing. I like to create uncomfortable moments between us because I find it can reveal a lot of truth.

I'll lie in bed with an awkward hard-on, pick up the phone, and inform someone that we just had transcendent sex in the ocean until we got twisted in kelp and drowned to orgasm. I have no qualms telling them that they just voted the Conservative Party of Canada into power for another term of total environmental devastation, or that they were dropped from a plane onto the roof of *le Stade*, bounced once, then punched through to their deaths. Their response is often silence. I'm used to it.

There's a recurring dream I often tell people about. Ever since I was a kid, about once a year I'll dream that my body levitates and starts to spin in slow orbit, just a few feet off the ground. I'm wrapped in a bed sheet and angled on an axis, rotating at an even speed. A perfect solstice. I watch myself from a distance, possibly separated from my body. There are variations of the dream where I'm cycling without a bike and manage to take off into the sky. Tripping over laundry and power lines, I can feel the power of flying. Maybe I just want to meet my friends somewhere other than on the bloody grounds of our daily lives. This dream elicits a number of interpretations. I consider them all before discarding.

But there is one dream I will never retell to the person involved. It's too infinite to articulate properly, too imprecise to read into, and too heartbreaking. Even a complete recounting here is out of the question.

It occurs somewhere on the meridian of sleep, the horizon of drifting away, a ledge I'm always about to fall off. Despite gravity, I manage to hang on to my perch. I get the twitches and breathe deeply, and then images erode my wakefulness and take over, a few blurry pixels at a time. I'm chained to a wall of ice. I seem to be in some kind of cavern as colourless as Lucite, cold but also fuzzy, the steam of condensation wrapped around me as I chill in the fridge, my prison. I don't know where my feet are. I assume my wrists are handcuffed in iron shackles, but it's hard to tell, because my hands and arms have gone numb. I know nothing about my situation, how I got here, how long I've been here, or how deep the cavern is. I just assume it goes on forever. Various moods visit me over time. They dervish around me like the smoke of dry ice and spirit away too quickly. Sometimes, when the condensation clears, I can make out long corridors; at other times, I'm convinced the cave is no more than a tiny box. Light illuminates my prison from different angles, sometimes piercing the floor, other times curling around a corner, but never directly from above. I've never liked overhead light, so I'm suspicious that I'm not subjected to it. Aren't dreams designed to torture you?

She starts to materialize. I don't see her, but I can hear her breathing, her hair swishing on the ice, the rattle of chains. It's the sound of rust falling and the rage of trying to break free. Sometimes I swear that I can hear tears rolling down her cheeks, freezing, then cracking and falling like tinkling ice chips. Uncertain music washes through the chamber. It drowns out the details about her movements that I struggle to make out. Is she in pain? Is she inching in my direction? Does she know I'm here? Am I where I think I am in relation to her body? Is she in her body when she shakes off the ice, or is she somewhere else, in another cold, distant shell? But I can't grasp her shape because the music separates us. It's a hard-core ambient wall of synth that makes me feel alone when I most need to feel connected. It lasts for hours.

Then I can be in the ice for weeks until I hear her again.

My days are filled with despair, with the understanding that there's no rescue, that I'm a child doomed to die of emotions frozen in time, choked by inactivity, lost to the world and forgotten by the compassionate, desperately clinging to any glint of light as a sign of hope, any disruption in the carpet of fog that has obscured my feet since I got here, so that I have no ground. All I want to do, aside from getting out of here, is lower my arms to my side. I would agree to live here forever if allowed to crouch for a few minutes.

I think I hear my name. I assume it's an illusion, but there it is again. She's calling me. She can't be far. But the music swells loud, and it's absolute pain. Shostakovich's Symphony no. 4 is a curtain of broken glass shattering the air, muffling voices, subsuming everything into the movement. I am lost in a cadence. Strangled by the necks of two French horns. Muted by *andante* overtones and a pressing hush. A mimic trumpet is camouflaged in her timbre, unmistakeable to my ears, but I am wounded in my confusion and granted a reprieve by a drop in the levels. And then completely lost in the atonal, sonic mud. Just another plaintive instrument fighting to be heard, I am. It echoes and echoes, and my name becomes unrecognizable. It becomes the middle part of a trombone solo I particularly hate.

The movement ends and the ice walls light up at once, as if my prison were on the inside of the sun and moving toward the inner surface, just under the brilliant mantle. At this speed, she could appear right in front of me; I'd recognize her anywhere. She's stranger than any symphony, that's obvious. We're two tortured spirits writhing helplessly in front of the other, a mutual display of ugliness. I think we're both naked. Elongated familial bones, sharing a marrow but on opposite sides of the chamber, our differences too slight to accept. How come we still can't touch each other? The lack of logic makes me shiver.

She's working her way free. Her mane of hair is caught in the ice, rays of light blasting through *rousse* and russet. She's a mosquito in the amber, escaping one strand at a time, twisting her head this way and that; her ice is melting, and her wet hair comes free—I can smell it—she smiles with every muscular yank of her neck, smiling high, she's working toward me—I can feel it—she hasn't looked at me yet, she's too busy breaking through the ice. Breaching. Her energy is what I've been waiting for. I open my hands to be held, open my heart to be rescued.

And I wait for her to look at me. But she doesn't.

Instead, she lurches out of the ice and forward. A wild woman, and all mine. She looks right through me, looks for the fastest way out.

All I have to say is "I'm here," but I can't say it.

All I have to do is open my mouth to let her see the shape of my teeth, leave a recognizable dental impression on her, but my mouth is sealed shut with ice.

All I have to do is scream internally to let her feel my vibration, and she'll press her warm body against my wall to melt it, enfold me into her, and make like old times. But my lungs are filled with crystals, so screaming just sounds like glass snapping one square centimetre at a time.

And then she, the only person I have ever seen in this ice chamber, up and leaves me all alone.

We were this close to escaping together, but I am stuck in this dream.

Fuck Shostakovich. Fuck ice.

IN ALL INNOCENCE

When you read out loud, do you see the same word twice?

Do the words jump around in your head?

Do you think clearly?

Do you think faster than your mouth is able to move?

Are you nervous?

Why don't you just slow down?

Why don't you think before you speak?

How come you don't practice the techniques you learned in therapy?

Were you dropped as a kid?

Have you ever thought it's because you're left-handed?

Are you doing it just to get attention?

How come sometimes you stutter and other times you don't?

Are you faking it to get out of doing stuff?

How could you forget your own name?

Why are you blinking your eyes like that?

Do you belong to a church that speaks in tongues?

Is it contagious?

Do you even stutter at all?

How many more assumptions about speech can you take?

What is your breaking point, and does it break on any word in particular?

MARILYN DOES MONTREAL

It was tough whenever we moved and I had to start a new school. There was a new class of thirty kids to become acquainted with, thirty new names to memorize. Of course, there were always two Stephens and two Michaels and up to three Christines and four Jessicas. So perhaps twenty-three new names to remember and match to the faces.

The memorizing was easy but the speaking wasn't. When addressing a classmate, I just used whatever name I could say at the moment. Because I had just moved to the neighbourhood and joined the school, I could use my newness as an excuse. I swapped Trevor with Nathan with Robert with Alicia with Rowena with Grace with Josh with Rodney with Sandra with impunity. I kept them straight in my head, but I kept them guessing in the aisles. Some of the kids started to wear name tags for my benefit, ones they glued to their shirts with spit. Or they would tell me their names every time we met. I think I got superficially high grades because the teachers pitied me for having what they thought was amnesia. That was kind of my style back then. I was a player well before I even had pubes. I was completely excused of the responsibility to remember. A Sun could very well be a Christophe. Perhaps I didn't even know what names I could say fluently. My feelings on the letter S were so hard to nail down on a sunny day in September when school started and I had to SSSSSSsssssssssss my way through everything. Who could pay attention under conditions like that, especially a slitherer like me?

Nobody wanted to sit beside me, and I knew why—I had the stink of a kid with a past. I could see them whispering to each other, trading versions of the same story. I guess word got around. Although even if it had happened, it didn't happen how they say it did.

I would sometimes fantasize about having a friend who was a boy, maybe a little older than me. We would ignore everybody else and have our own fun. I drew pictures of him in my notebook and gave him a name: Derek. We would skip school to go skating on Beaver Lake, then eat lunch outside and huff on each other's hands with peanut butter breath to keep them warm. We'd jump the fence at the railway tracks, even though there was a hole big enough to crawl through. Just to be different. When a train passed, Derek and I would shake our dicks at it and laugh and laugh, just two boys flopping a weird signal to the conductor in unison. Maybe that was something that boys could do together.

Derek would pretend not to know that I stuttered. He would find a reason not to hear it.

I drew him over and over.

The homeroom teacher was just another strange man in my life who asked me the weirdest questions. Where was Chibougamau? Were the Iroquois hunters or gatherers? In what year was Nouvelle-France founded? I found it odd how he always wore the tightest possible pants, almost as if he were trying to teach us the shape of the Gaspé Peninsula, a quick geography lesson enhanced by well-placed fabric.

What territory borders Quebec to the northeast and is directly above the Gaspé?

Newfoundland.

In some respects, yes. But more officially?

Nitassinan.

Excuse me?

It's land taken from the Innu, and they never said we could.

You're avoiding my question.

I answered it.

Why don't you just say what it's called in your damn textbook?

Two Jessicas raised their hands to answer the question. The Jessicas always had the answer. But the teacher had this way of ignoring student participation by pretending to look for hands and then, seeing none, feigning near-sightedness when it was a deliberate act of blindness. He let the Jessica hands wilt on the vine. We watched them fall in disappointment.

Well, it's kind of the shape of *that thing* you've got there, so if I said the word, I'd be in trouble.

The class laughed. I knew the teacher was going to make me pay for that remark. I could feel the full weight and heft of his retribution coming at me in slow motion, ever closer as the laughter died down and we could all see the meanness in his face. I was about to get demolished by the nastiest homeroom teacher this side of the Miron gravel quarry. I suddenly pictured myself dead at the bottom of the pit, a pile of boy bones that the city vultures picked clean. This vulture swooped in too coolly. It knew exactly what it was doing.

Say it.

Why are you asking me if you already know?

Because it's your job as a student to say it, not mine. If you don't say it, everyone here will get detention tonight. Every. Single. One. Now, do you want that? Do they want that?

Game changer. I could feel the allegiance of the class suddenly shift. They dropped me. Self-interest and the prospect of a lost hour had cost me the kids who, a few seconds prior, had been so impressed with my wit. I felt heavier; my ass was cemented to the wooden seat, my tongue even harder to lift. I resigned myself to my fate. As always, that fate was whatever unimaginable future awaited me at the start of a word.

Say it.

L-L-L-ubbock.

Yes, it's Lubbock, Texas. Neighbouring Quebec. A-plus for that.

L-L-L-L-▮

I blocked. So typical of me. A block is ugly to watch—my jaw seizes up, forcing my lips together. The word literally has nowhere to go. The pressure deforms the lower half of my face. Enter the freak.

We won't judge you. Just go ahead and say it.

I felt all the students' eyes fixate on my mouth and throat, students who probably imagined throttling me if squeeze came to choke. Eight eyes of Jessica, six retinas of Christine, and at least eight sets of Michael eyelashes. It was in these moments—when I took a hard look, not just at them and our brutish and sadistic leader, but at the classroom itself, the stupid art projects on the wall beside the fundraising thermometers coloured in with marker, the stupid snowflake cut-outs, the stupid everything—that I wondered if I even belonged there, if they even deserved to hear my answer, if it wasn't easier for me to move to another school, pack up our apartment into boxes. I could imagine moving as the easier alternative to answering the question, but of course, I had no packing tape, no boxes, no X-Acto knives, no markers, and ultimately, no place to go. Anywhere I travelled would be territory alien to the terrain of my mouth. I would always be unwelcome. So while my body stood still, my mind wandered to these forbidden, unspeakable places.

You must really want to spend the rest of your afternoon in detention. Maybe we'll even throw in some extra homework for everybody.

L-L-L-sorry-L-llllllllll

Are you waiting for help? Should I reach into your mouth and pull it out for you? Come on, you can push it out yourself, you're a big boy.

L-Labrador.

Brilliant! Now kids, *that's* how you put on a show.

I was always so freaked out by classroom experiences that I ran to the arcade afterward to lose myself for awhile. I wasn't very good at video games, so I stuck to the easy ones, the ones where you shot random animals in the face and made their brains explode on heavily pixilated scenery. Their heads were so big, you just couldn't miss. The moose made giant splats.

So I was always late to see Rosa, my speech therapist who worked at the Montreal Children's Hospital.

That day, she sat me down in front of her and started our session with a physical treatment. She wrapped her hands around my neck, gently at first. Then she started rolling it like a pat of dough. As she twisted, I could almost feel my neck growing longer, my head extending further from my shoulders. While she massaged my jaw muscles, I looked down to see my body far below. Maybe that was how a giraffe saw the world. (As a dog boy, I would never know.) I cleared my throat and felt new space opening up, a hollowness I wondered how to fill. That's when I began to suspect that words got bigger when you got older, that they needed more room inside you.

It was always comforting to see her silver curls, the warmth of her smile, the sureness of her touch. At the time, I thought she lived at the hospital. After all, it was very homey (there was a rug, sofa, and TV), and she was always brewing tea. Looked like a living room to me.

She felt my voiced and non-voiced breath to make sure I was doing it right. I spent my childhood in this loving stranglehold, this embrace, my veins reddening to the touch. I wondered if some kids were freaked out when an adult did this. I was always at ease with it. It actually relaxed me to the point of sleepiness. I stared at her silver hair and was mesmerized in the gleam until it all became blurry and my eyes started to close.

How was school?

Huh? Oh, fine.

That doesn't sound fine to me.

It was okay. Just stupid.

I see. Have you been using the techniques we practiced?

Yes.

And how do they work out for you?

I don't want to say.

Why not?

Because if I say the truth then you'll feel bad.

You can be open with me.

Okay. Well, like, it's really hard? It's hard enough to think about *what* I'm trying to say, never mind *how* I'm saying it. Know what I mean? I'm not sure if that makes sense.

I know it's hard. That's why I'm helping you.

And um, um, um, um, sorry—even if I did, um, practice, and it came out smoothly, nobody would know how much work it took to get it out.

It's normal to want to feel appreciated. You could tell them about our visits.

Tell them about you?

Yes.

And us?

You seem shocked. There are far stranger things than what you and I do together. Do you think they would make fun of you? Is that it, sweetie?

What I was thinking but didn't want to tell her is that they wouldn't believe she was real. By that point in my life, I had already experienced enough heartbreak about people assuming I had imaginary friends. I didn't want Rosa to fall into that category, so I figured it was best never to mention her to anybody.

The techniques. Most were innocuous, if a little oddball.

Sometimes she made me hum to myself through a bendable straw connecting my mouth to my ear. Mostly, I heard the music of drool. That was fine. She would take notes in a scrawl I couldn't read. But there were stranger techniques. She made me realize that when I hit words head on, they blocked. So she presented a way for me to soften my approach, to avoid attacking them: Come to the first word of a sentence in a long, slow breath. A constant stream of air. Lips don't touch. Blow it out sultry. Blow it out like Marilyn.

Those Montreal summers in the 1980s, my lips became two strips of red velvet. At first, I was drop-dead serious about the therapy. I practiced the techniques and started to take care of my lips. I applied cherry lip balm all the fucking time. Part of my practice involved having conversations with strangers on the street; I had to buy a copy of the *Montreal Daily News*, ask about Metro fare, and deal with strange men. I had to give them my best Marilyn Monroe, I mean, whatever I said, it must've sounded like I was asking for a cigarette and a lift. I did my sultry little boy routine all across town, bouncing my imaginary blond curls in their faces. With every breathy inquiry, I called them "mister." They stared at my shiny red lips that were always slightly parted, always about to say something. I made many new friends that summer. Montreal was mine, but I was a rather nervous bombshell. I'm sure some people assumed I had a breathing problem because on several occasions I was offered an inhaler.

I had telephone exercises as well. I'd have to call a place of business and ask three rehearsed questions. Sometimes I got really nervous and mixed the questions up. I'd call the *bibliothèque* and ask them to reserve a table for me and my wife. I'd ask Revenu Québec what time the next flight left for Baltimore. I drew all my words out in sexy moans. One time, I called Birks to ask for a diamond necklace that I could wear to *l'Orchestre symphonique de Montréal* that night—since I was the esteemed guest of Maître Charles Dutoit—and of course, if someone could come to my hotel the next morning to collect the used merchandise. They actually thought I was Marilyn Monroe. I told them she was dead. That I was dead. They said they knew all along that the suicide was a cover. I hung up the phone as fast as my sticky impostor fingers could drop the receiver.

Sometimes I made an unscheduled call to Rosa, so I could test the doctor's medicine on the doctor herself.

Hello?

Don't ask me why I'm calling, gorgeous. Ask me when I'm going to hang up.

Who is this?

We were in a picture together. Doncha remember, baby? When I kissed you, I made you know it was for real. But they wouldn't let us kiss anymore, so we beat it. We beat it, baby, and never came back. Do you know who this is now?

How could I forget?

That's what I mean. You don't forget dynamite. But here's the thing. I'm getting sick of this town. We need a new one where we can be gorgeous.

I assume you have a plan for that.

Sure do, but you gotta shut up about it.

You can trust me.

Do you know how to drive stick? I like to see my old l-l-l-lllllady behind the wheel.

That sounds fine, but can you remember to breathe?

Click.

I hung up on Rosa so I could unleash a stream of pent-up stutters, jerking and bobbing and convulsing in the corner for a full minute, some of which was pleasurably silent.

It was really hard to keep the Marilyn act up. It was easier for me to stutter than to enact my fluency tools, so I eventually let them drop. I'm sure that, to Rosa, it seemed my stuttering got worse during our time together. That was exactly what I'd expected: I've always stuttered heavily around people I'm most comfortable with because I feel I can be myself with them. And don't you want to be comfortable around your therapist? Oh, well. Every industry has its built-in paradoxes. I eventually let Rosa drop. Maybe I'd never outgrow my voice, but I definitely outgrew the Montreal Children's Hospital.

There was one thing that really made me question my decision to leave, however: Rosa was the only adult, aside from the Grand Antonio, who ever bought my dog act. If I was thirsty, she'd fill a metal bowl with water and place it on the floor. She'd scratch me roughly behind the ears while I dozed on a cushion in the sun. She'd blow a dog whistle for a few minutes before our sessions, knowing I'd hear it when I came bounding up the stairs. When I galloped through nearby Cabot Square, the spaniels, terriers, and setters would be yipping on high alert. Thankfully, they only let biped German Shepherds into the hospital.

On our last visit, I stole the dog whistle that was on her desk.

Another year went by, and I grew even more uncertain. How long could a Marilyn creature last in a world as brutal as this one without breaking? How long could a boy go misunderstood? How much pretending until I bought my own act and excused myself from reality? How many years would it take for us to accept that we're all butterflies with wings so mismatched that camouflage is impossible? That no matter how deep the snow gets, we'll never learn to lift our feet high enough? Strangely, these were the uncertainties that kept me trotting, one paw after the other.

There were only a few unquestionable facts.

For instance, if I was a dog, I wasn't a Labrador.

E = MJ SQUARED

After these things I saw, and, look! a great crowd, which no man was able to number, out of all nations and tribes and peoples and tongues, standing before the throne and before the Lamb, dressed in white robes; and there were palm branches in their hands.

—REVELATION 7:9

It's true, my favourite lyrics were written by the prophets. I'd go to *le Stade* to hear them. The summer District Convention of Jehovah's Witnesses was always good for a performance. I'd sit and listen to speeches about the Book of Revelation, about the seven-headed wild beast, all muscles and testicles, slicked and oiled horns at least nine smooth inches of solid length. We followed along in a book with illustrations. The beast waged war with body-building angels, packages bulging through their tunics, hard-ons for the righteousness of Jehovah's Kingdom. They wrestled and fought until they were covered in each other's sweat, tears, and spit, a roiling mass of hotness until, a few Bible passages and illustrations later, we, the teenagers sitting under the semi-retracted stadium roof pinched together imperfectly like a wrinkled scrotum, couldn't tell good and evil apart, the beasts from the angels.

Sometimes we, the teenagers, needed to excuse ourselves to the bathroom.

On one such pleasure trip, I wandered a little too far. I went past the bleachers and into the bowels of *le Stade*, into the dark service corridors where water rotted the concrete and lime seeped through, where tiny mineral stalactites caught the flashlight beams that the clueless security guards waved in my direction but somehow never shone directly on me. I roamed farther away from Jehovah and deeper into the heart of this building I loved. These were the paths that the superstars travelled on their way to the stage or the baseball field, I thought. I tried to feel the silence just before the roar, just before the spotlights hit. I found an unopened CroBar on the ground—a candy bar honouring the Expos' very own Warren Cromartie. Rumour was that proceeds went to juvenile diabetes. I was happy that adults were always thinking of kids that way. I stuffed the seven inches into my face and promised myself I'd never get the affliction.

I wandered farther backstage to get some alone time with my book so I could fawn over an illustration, an image of Moses leading his people through the desert. Windswept, sunburnt, all bent out of fashion, yet resilient. A creature of the sand. It is said that he had an "infirmity of speech," and I was proud of that, proud that we shared a trait so many centuries apart. I felt like I knew him, could connect with him through the pages. How did he routinely address thousands of people huddled in sandstorms? Did the sand not steal a single word he didn't steal from himself? The mystery of a mouth held sway over me. He wasn't the first stutterer I ever knew, but he was still a role model.

In the dark stadium guts, I gazed lovingly at Moses.

When I heard footsteps approaching, I thought I recognized the sound of his sandals. But then I saw that the footfalls belonged to a stick-like man with a sure gait, impeccably groomed, with skinny black flood pants, cocaine-white spats of a regal nature, a human nature, midnight-black silk chemise covered in rhinestones chiselled to catch the sharpest edges of shadow, curls that covered his face, and a brimmed hat that covered the curls. He looked down and walked forward with tap-dance clicks that echoed in the depths of the cavern until I thought I would go deaf.

Of course, it was Michael Jackson, a former member of our flock. Seeing him immediately brought a scripture to mind:

> *Look! He is coming with the clouds, and every eye will see him, and those who pierced him; and all the tribes of the earth will beat themselves in grief because of him. Yes, Amen.* —REVELATION 1:7

The most famous Jehovah's Witness of all, the closest we ever got to a flesh-and-blood saviour. His fall from Jehovah's grace started with his video for "Thriller," which the Witnesses accused of promoting the occult—a no-no, according to what we were taught. Then they printed a grovelling and probably fabricated apology from Michael in *Awake!* magazine promising never to do it again. Who makes the greatest music video ever and then disowns it?

It's just not done. (Besides, when you throw zombies under the bus, they don't die.) When MJ later disassociated himself from the organization, I was relieved, because I knew that he would pour his anger into music, and that it would be great.

I couldn't help but ask what he was doing there. I suspected that either he was trying to catch echoes of his Victory Tour performance at *le Stade* several years prior, or he was planning to take the stage at the District Convention to reclaim the hearts of Jehovah's people—the only fans he has ever truly cared about—with choreography that was so stunning and unprecedented that the Witnesses could only interpret it as prophecy and be forced to take him back. He confirmed one of my suspicions.

Oh, hi. I'm just...I'm just, you know, rehearsing for my new show.

What's it called?

It doesn't have a title yet. Still figuring out the dance moves. Then the music will come, I guess. I was wondering...I don't know, it's just an idea...do you want to be in it?

Um, sure thing, Michael Jackson. Why not. But what would I do?

Whatever you want.

I could be a dog. Hey, I can lap a gallon of water in under forty seconds! Not just any mutt can do that.

Oh wow, that sounds wonderful. You could totally be our new dog. Hey, you want to see a new move? I've been working on something. It's just...it's just that it's not ready yet, so I hope you understand. I hope you like it.

Of course. I'm sure I'll like it. Show me.

That's when I saw the King of Pop move like water slipping through concrete. He melted into a shape I couldn't process and moved around me to an indefinite beat, a fractional time signature, elbows where knees should be, ankles and wrists switched on the joint; he enveloped me like a wraith, graced me with cool air from all sides, wobbled me into imitations of the movement, but they were slightly too sophisticated for a boy still becoming a phantom. So even though I witnessed him become time itself, time that slowed down, a theory of dance relativity in which everything passes more slowly for a body in motion than one in stasis, I still missed everything.

MJ finished on an uncertain hover. He leaned against a wall. I lobbed a soft question at him to make sure he was actually there.

Isn't anyone looking for you?

Probably the same people who are looking for you, kid. Nobody right now. Enjoy it. I gotta go. It's been real, real nice chatting with you. It's just…it's just that…

And he was gone. I was alone with the stalactites.

I could feel that he had come to deliver a message to me. But what exactly? As the Armageddon clouds begin to dissipate, I wondered…would I become an ex-Jehovah's Witness like him when I grew up?

Sometimes the students teased me when I brought my JW literature to school. I should've known better than that! High schools in Montreal's West Island were the coolest in the city. You couldn't simply read a *Watchtower* magazine in the cafeteria and expect to get away with it.

In my high school, everyone always practiced their cement face.

Indifferent to drama, they let it all bounce off an expressionless façade. It was the uninterested look they gave when a math teacher told off a student for not being top form on quadratic equations, or when a gym teacher explained Sex Ed through overly vigorous pushups. It was a fascist neutrality.

The students practiced cement face on each other too. If someone said something shocking—like the reason they smelled is because they had just finished fucking a fellow tenth grader to Nirvana's *Nevermind*, or equally as shocking, that they were still a virgin, or if they revealed that their parents were millionaires and several castes above the rest of us, or conversely, too poor to afford a grad photo—the surrounding faces gave nothing away. The trouble with cement face is that it could appear too disapproving or moody, which had social implications. The key was to open your eyes a little wider while giving the face. It required a muscular awareness that could only be attained by practicing in mirrors hung on the insides of locker doors. You just had to remember that everything was reversed in the mirror.

Sometimes, students accidentally gave each other cement face in the mirror. Fellow practitioners of the art could easily recognize each other. We were as remote as the suburbs in which we lived. Nothing could impress us. We expressed no emotion while storms brewed inside.

Kids in grades seven and eight often let their frustration slip through cracks in the face—a flared nostril, quivering lip, redness. They paid for this laziness by making themselves prey. The older kids feasted on the reactions of the young, grew full on their shock. There were so many things you could say to someone to make their mouth fall slightly open, to make them look away, bite their lip, frown. Sometimes the younger kids thought they were doing cement face. They stood still, but didn't realize their cheeks were livid palettes of emotion, morphing as feelings raced through them and toppled each other. It was ugly but delicious. The grade ten vultures were trained to spot the mannerisms of the weak, the give-aways of the soon-to-be-dead.

We had other problems. Acne interfered in a major way with social domination. The millionaires among us spent thousands on Oxy cleansers, Neutrogena, and other skin-clearing agents. The poor among us wiped their oily faces on their T-shirts. We all did something to get rid of the zits and blackheads that marred our otherwise perfectly bland faces.

I had fantasized about having a cement face, but stuttering made that impossible. I clenched my teeth and contorted my lips through every other sentence, as if my face were the surface of a massage chair and my words the rotors just underneath that warped the surface. Time froze when I did that, and everyone looked. Some kids made fun of me for bloodsport, but others admired me for having the nerve to show my storms. At first, I was confused and wondered how they could think I would stutter on purpose. They reminded me that I chose to speak. In our high school, I had the option of not saying anything at all. You could coast wordlessly through five years, and nobody would know. My choice impressed some people. But I still wasn't invited to cement-face parties, which were basically students milling around looking at each other's teenage stone, masquerade balls of kids disguised in the thinnest of antibacterial wipes. What was everyone so afraid of? We were all assholes.

The most visible thing on my face at all times, however, was desire. Sex had started to spring in me like a slow leak, one that didn't release any of the pressure. Gym class appeared to be an intricately designed form of torture for young queers. The definition of wrestling appeared to be a guy straddling your head so that when you tried to catch your breath, your nostrils vacuumed up his nuts, and his scent defeated you. I'd run home to beat off to Vanilla Ice, stretched out on the bed with my undies around my ankles and headphones clasped on my head like the big, warm hands of a hung teen wrestler making me submit.

Music always turned me on—that was a given. But it gave me subtler messages, too. For example, that there were shadows in my past connected to music, and possibly even to particular songs. I would have to turn my life into a playlist and listen for the minor keys, the mistakes. I would have to transform the darkness into sex so I could understand it on the physical plane, because sex was something I wanted to make more knowable to myself.

I suppose it was a coincidence that when I went to the HMV music store and squatted at a listening booth, ready for a few hours of discovery, "Beat It" was the next cued song. But that would surely be jumping ahead—I decided to start my search with songs beginning with the letter A. Cue the start of a long and boring future.

Most of the music sucked. That's probably why I started a band. My real friends were good to me. Outcasts never admit to their shared failures, they just cling to each other. For whatever reason, we hopped a bus at Fairview mall one day and went downtown to Steve's Music. We spent the rest of our acne budget on amplifiers and guitars, electric and acoustic, steel and nylon strings. Maybe we'd need an egg shaker, so might as well pick one up, and a Casio keyboard with pre-programming to make up for the years of music lessons we didn't take, and maybe we could get that drum kit if they accepted us for the layaway program. Luckily, back then our parents wrote their PIN numbers on the backs of their debit cards. Easy theft. Loaded with our new gear, we couldn't get on the Metro, the bus wouldn't take us, and fucked if we were going to spring for a taxi van, since the surcharge was a rip-off. Hitchhiking from downtown back to the West Island with our swag made us feel like a real band. I suppose that, technically, it was the first and last time we were ever on tour.

With the help of a few chord charts, and after stealing licks—if not note-for-note then at least in spirit and posturing—from the Cure, the Smiths, Pink Floyd, the Tragically Hip, the Cult, and Depeche Mode, we started to entertain each other in a basement studio deep in the West Island bedrock. I'm pretty sure that the harder and louder we flailed, and the more electricity we wasted, blasting our inexperience and lack of musical prowess to nobody, deaf to each other's atonal meanderings and timing mistakes, the deeper we sank into the rock. We expected record executives to hear us through the stone and come knocking with a record deal.

Our careers took a turn during one of those sessions. The drummer missed his last cymbal crash by at least half a foot. Time for a break. We made sure there was a towel under the basement door. The windows were open and the driveway was empty. We smoked a spliff and talked about making an album, getting on university radio stations like Montreal's very own CKUT, and maybe even into the pages of *Chart Magazine*, Canada's alternative music monthly.

Pretty sure we could knock Treble Charger and Sloan to the back pages. Our guitar virtuoso skipped his toke to lay something heavy on me, something that would forever pit us against each other, and unfortunately, completely alter the history of unheard pop music.

You should be our singer.

Um, you're joking. We don't even have a mic.

Yeah, we do, we just never took it out of the box. It's over there.

Uh...why me?

Because it makes sense. You've been writing lyrics.

How do you know?

It doesn't matter.

It matters. And they're not really lyrics. They're more like poems. They have nothing to do with our songs.

We can make them fit. That's how bands do it. Everyone knows that Cobain wrote "Something in the Way" as a suicide note, and when Nirvana just happened to find it, he pretended it was for one of the songs. You can tell when he sings the part about fish not having any feelings. Nothing fits. Get it? That's it. Anyways, you have nice hair.

And singing is about having nice hair?

Someone has to get the rest of us laid. It doesn't really matter who. But we do need someone.

I suppose I could give it a try.

If you were planning to do anything to yourself, like bad stuff, you'd tell us, right? Some of your lyrics are kind of...

Stop going through my fucking stuff. The weed is making you paranoid.

In our haste to make the cover of *Chart Magazine*, we forgot to buy a mic stand, so we ended up crazy-gluing the mic to the top of a tall blue bong we placed on a table. We got the microphone to work, somewhat, despite bad feedback. I stepped up with a sheet of looseleaf in hand, suddenly relieved of my keyboard responsibilities. I opened my mouth and sang.

It was the first time I could ever remember not stuttering for entire minutes at a time. It was weird to be so unbroken. I should've been happy. Really happy. But I could see my reflection in the blue bong glass, and soon sank into a musical depression that, as it turns out, was perfect for the song. Because what I saw was cement face. I was giving it. And it was terrible, because I suddenly didn't belong with my friends. Wearing this new face, I belonged with the strangers at school whom I could never know, and who could never know me. I vowed never to sing again.

That was the beginning of the end of the greatest band never to come out of the West Island. We became an instrumental group. I started to write lyrics in French, and kept them to myself:

Dieu le roi

L'ange de nos ruelles froides

Embrasse-nous, écrase-nous

Tes enfants fidèles

Tes enfants grands et curieux

Explique-nous la guerre

Explique-nous les cris d'animaux si forts

Si forts partout

Champion du monde

Sacré coeur, coeur géant

Antonio de Rosemont

Force des forces
Ange des trottoirs, Dieu le roi

ERIC

CRIES AND WHISPERS

It was my summer of New Order. I went through their entire catalogue, not just the greatest hits collection *Substance* or even the extensive *John Peel Sessions,* but rather, all the albums and singles and imports and rare pressings. I wanted to hold time inside me in some way, to collect it and feel its movement, its passage through my body.

Mostly, I wanted something impossible. I wanted to feel the exact moment that Joy Division became New Order. I knew in my heart that the death of Ian Curtis wasn't the only dividing line, that in electronic music there was more grey than black and white. So I dissected the discography into thousands of little pieces in my head, trying to detect the changes in tone, in melody, in meaning. I was pretty sure I had stumbled upon something significant when I learned that the song "Mesh" was mislabelled "Cries and Whispers" on most releases of *Substance,* while the song "Cries and Whispers" was nowhere on the record. On cassette versions, the song "Cries and Whispers" appeared, but it was mislabelled "Mesh." What was the true relationship of these two tracks? What was the hidden intention behind these calculated flubs? It sent my brain spinning into conspiracies that explained the 1990s as they had so far unravelled, and held predictions for the end of the decade. All I knew is that one thing unlocked the other, and vice versa, and if I could study the pattern, the teeth on the keys in the lock, then I could learn to apply the model to the aspects of my life that needed locksmithing.

What I couldn't process or handle was the news that some releases had the song "Mesh" labelled "Mesh (Cries and Whispers)." It was clear that someone was deliberately trying to fuck with me.

I spent time working these details out and drinking myself silly at loft parties in Griffintown, where everyone had a 3,000-square-foot space with sixteen-foot ceilings, and the rent was something like $500, but nobody knew exactly who lived there or how to pay the landlord because there was a good chance that the building was abandoned and the tenants were squatters. There were always ecstasy pills between the sofa cushions, and crabs and scabies. But at least there was ecstasy. When the cops came to kick us out at three a.m. because some asshole neighbour complained about the noise, we'd stumble over to Stornoway Gallery to see if the painters had any drugs, and since they had taken them all, we just made out with them, hoping to get stoned on their saliva.

Eric and I met at one of these parties, held in a loft. It was a rave, but nobody called it that. What a strange American word for a bunch of Montreal fleabags like us who got together to split our drugs and drink for as cheaply as possible away from home. I didn't see anything marketable in our nighttime activities, but a rave it was, and it was catching. The night we met, I had downed a six-pack of Dow beer from Quatres Frères and puffed through half a pack of Peter Stuyvesants. I stopped to pick up an extra pack before the party. The loft was full of the usual neighbourhood freaks, including some boys who had fucked me, but thankfully they were too wasted to recognize me, and I could dance in peace. Pet Shop Boys and Violent Femmes, I think. Then someone jammed two fingers into my nostrils and mainlined me with Vicks VapoRub. My nasal passages exploded with eucalyptus and cherry mint, and my lungs opened up wide, giving me an oxygen rush. Then I saw the boy attached to the fingers, but before I could say anything, he stuffed a Ring Pop candy pacifier into my mouth, lime flavour. We danced on a compound sugar high until morning. I yelled at him above the music, and he just nodded at whatever I said. I was so attracted to how close he stood to the rack of subwoofers, so fearless. We made out for hours, a sloppy mess of cisgender privilege.

After a while he said he had to go, leaving me confused and with a boner. We didn't have a pen, so I made him scratch his number into the foil wrapper on my pack of smokes. Then some real good shit came on, I think it was Duran Duran. I couldn't stop my body from moving, but I was terrified of accidentally flattening his number out of the foil. Still, I said fuck it and danced as hard as the music made me.

The next day, I could hardly make out the number, but there it was. I took a chance and called him. Whoever answered hung up. I tried again and got more hang-ups. Morning-after remorse? I tried not to take it personally, and for me, that meant getting my drinking on early. Luckily, the *dépanneur* on the corner opened at ten a.m. on Sunday, which meant I could get a bottle of Baby Duck red wine in exchange for beer empties. You knew it was a good wine just by smelling the inside of the twist-off cap. It went particularly well with my classy Peter Stuyvesants.

Home was on rue Prince Arthur, a seven-room flophouse on top of a Portuguese restaurant, a hundred bucks a month, but nobody had the money. Nobody could remember ever seeing the lease. We lived in the luxury of our opulent squalor. Each roommate had their own radically different aesthetic, so we violently co-existed side-by-side in the two-floor museum of clashing styles, from the baroque student-poverty look, to dilapidated IKEA showroom, to *Trainspotting* smackhouse grey, to classic Persian in felted red and gold gilt. Each of our private spaces was a vomiting of our ideals. For people sharing a house, we couldn't have been more different. My own look involved throwing everything out except for a giant oak desk with copper-riveted green leather trim and a chair placed at the other end of the room. I was going for the sparse Soho gallery look.

There was a living room in the house, but we suspected the furniture of harbouring a dormant army of scabies mites, so we avoided it. Instead, the kitchen became our communal space, with no decoration other than the two-year pile-up of unwashed glasses and dishes filled with cigarette ash. Some of that mess pre-dated us, so no one took responsibility.

The kitchen was an anti-design zone. One day, when everyone was out, Jack had the brilliant idea to make fries, as if you couldn't buy them from any number of places down the block. He started a grease fire, resulting in a ten-foot swath of charcoal soot on the ceiling. Jack was an artist looking for a gallery (weren't we all), so before anyone came home to see the damage, he decided to decorate the singular black column with arabesque strokes of mascara, a fresco that supposedly told the story of humanity as smoke marching through the ages.

We had no problem with the fire, but the art was hideous. We group-evicted him within the hour, everything straight from the second-floor window.

The kitchen was where we sat and commiserated about our romantic failures, our near hook-ups. It was the room where there were always spare cigarettes on the table. We ate McCain Deep'n Delicious frozen chocolate cheesecake right out of the pan for all-nighter breakfast and planned the next night's crash and burns. We were a crusty facsimile of the Golden Girls, promising to be there for each other the following morning, which was just a continuation of the previous night, with reheated coffee from recycled grounds brewed through the pantyhose of excommunicated roommates. We had no sense of time. The kitchen was the room where we talked about HIV and AIDS and seroconversion and what people were saying about the new drug cocktails. It was where we learned the vocabulary to describe friends who were disappearing, either literally or because stigma made them invisible. Maybe stigma killed them, too.

Rumour had it that our place was an old headquarters of *le Front de la libération du Québec*. We could feel the FLQ history in our kitchen, the desperate drags and hauls taken late into the night, the anguish of revolution permanently staining the ceiling. We fantasized that our table was where they dreamed up the kidnappings of James Cross and Pierre Laporte—and who knows who else? What a morbid honour.

When I got home after the rave, one of my roommates, Ingenue, could tell that something was wrong. No one was really sure how Ingenue came to live there, they just showed up on the couch one day and handed me a hundred dollars. It was the first of the month. Ingenue may have been the only one to *ever* pay rent on time. This earned them a certain unshakeable mystique. Their look helped with that: press-on cow eyelashes about four inches long, tube dress made of black electrical tape, and Air Jordans that they constantly pumped.

I told Ingenue the story of my lost boy, and they moved their chair in front of mine, interrogation-style. Ingenue took out a sketchpad and started to draw a face.

Tell me, sister. What does he look like?

Like an asshole. Draw an asshole where his nose should be.

Sounds like he's the perfect face-fuck. Get in that. Or I will. But seriously, what does his hair look like?

Dirty blond and always in my face.

Always in your face…like this?

Yeah. Round chin but square jaw, can suck a pacifier really, really well. Honestly, I'm seeing this all through club light, but I think he had green eyes and sort of orange fffffffffffffffffffffffffff-ff-fff-sorry-fff, um, you know, like orange dots on his nose.

Sweetie.

Yes.

You apologize every time you stutter. Don't you realize that's your special power? That most of us dream of having a power like that? Never apologize for your stuttering. It makes the rest of us feel like shit, takes away our hope. And honestly, boyfriend, it makes you look like a privileged fucking cunt.

Sorry. Whatever you say.

No, you're not sorry.

Uh, right.

So you were saying. Green eyes?

Yeah. But does that even make a difference? You're using a pencil.

Is this him?

Ingenue turned their sketchpad to me so I could see their rendition of Eric. It was bang-on. I was surprised to see him wearing a T-shirt on which was written his phone number, in jumbled order, along with a floating question mark, but that was him, standing cool, with his zipper undone, and dripping sex. The strangest part of the image was the backdrop. I could tell by the surrounding buildings that he was standing in the train yards in Pointe-Saint-Charles, close to the tracks. And his eyes were closed. I was perplexed.

What's wrong? That's him, isn't it?

Um, yeah. But why is he there?

Dove, you said when you kissed him it felt like your gums meshed together, right? That you traded a gallon of saliva, and you could taste his loneliness, and when he pulled away it was only because of the sacred primacy of music, he had to dance it out, and that you figured you'd be coming home together last night, right? Right?

Weird, I never said that. Now that I remember, though, I told him to meet me outside, yeah.

But he didn't. God, can we do something about that shit on the ceiling? It's giving me shingles. And then when you called today, he hung up on you. You called back and he hung up again, right?

Y-yy-y-y- mhmm. I mean, yeah.

Then he's in the train yard.

Right now?

Listen, I have to go. I'm not your fucking psychic. I'm doing a Crystal Waters cabaret at World Beat tonight. It's a contest. I'm going to own that fucking bitch.

With that, Ingenue got up, sang and shimmied the opening bars to "Gypsy Woman," and left me there with my bottle of Baby Duck, an ashtray full of questions, and the drawing of Eric. I had a boner to take care of so I got dressed—as Johnny Cash put it so well in his song "Sunday Morning Coming Down," in "my cleanest dirty shirt"—and headed to the Metro where I tried to negotiate about the fare. If the landlord could wait, why couldn't they? No dice. Maybe they didn't like the open bottle of wine. So I left the Metro and walked through the horror of downtown, the disgusting crowds of morning people dressed in bright colours, the putrid sun. Thank god for my sunglasses. When a night creature walks through the day, they walk alone.

I found Eric by the tracks. I compared him to Ingenue's sketch a few times, and, yep, but his back was turned to me. I had the sudden idea that we were both sleepwalkers and not awake, the somnambulant who have lost their way out of nightclubs, looking for misplaced drugs, perhaps stumbling to take a piss or wander from bed to bed, and we get caught in these ugly daytime positions against our will. Luckily, we don't remember any of it.

I called Eric's name, but he didn't turn around. Like he hung up on me again. Or did I have the wrong name? I yelled a little louder, and when I did, a train barrelled by, the steel wheels screaming the cry of morning so loud, so brash, I covered my ears, but he just stood there and soaked it in, let the rumble fill his body. And then I understood that he heard through vibration.

After the train had passed, he turned around and saw me. I was still calling his name, as if wishing my mouth to be the reason he'd quaked on the edge of the ties.

We walked back to the Plateau together, sharing a single pair of sweaty sunglasses. Taking turns. Halfway back to Prince Arthur, he lifted my arm, stuck his nose into my pit hair, and took a good raunchy whiff.

I forgot to ask Ingenue what their special power was.

THE MILLIPEDE

Eric is deaf.

He says it's not an impairment to him, just a quiet space some-where behind the senses. He says being deaf doesn't mean there's no sound in his head. He says he can hear music as well as I do, just differently. Eric says a lot of things.

But I don't believe him that it's fine, that he doesn't want to hear again. I know he knows what he's missing, that he's never heard the emotion in my voice, the sound of my key in the lock, the sound of me turning to him in the dark and saying something intimate just before sleep. It has been years since he's heard the sound of a dog drinking water, David Bowie caterwauling, or Tina Turner telling us why heroes are unnecessary. I refuse to believe he doesn't wish for these things.

So I forgive myself for pitying him. I forgive myself for dream-ing about hearing restoration surgery that neither of us can afford because we're young and poor. I forgive myself for wanting some-thing for him that he doesn't want. I forgive myself for thinking selfishly, because one day there will be a song I really, really need him to hear.

You might say that to compensate for his deafness, and perhaps out of protest, I indulge my own sense of hearing.

We moved in together a few months after meeting. Our new apartment didn't sound like other apartments. Nobody does acoustics like me. I wallpapered because I found the unadorned walls too sonically reflective of cutlery clatter. I chinked my closet with expanding builder's foam when I twigged that the downstairs neighbour had a habit of falling asleep in front of the news and the sound came up through the floorboards. I disabled the doorbell so people had to knock, and I padded the front door with soft foam so they had to knock quietly. I regularly oiled every door hinge.

It took me forever to figure out how to place our stereo speakers just right. They couldn't be facing each other, nor could they be facing away. I learned and internalized the concept of "toeing in" wherein the lava of sound is directed at the listener to form an equilateral triangle, which helps to avoid distortion. The speakers point at the ears of the listener. The third ear completes the triangle. Move your head back a few inches, and the music will disappear completely. Enjoy the mystery. Headphones are an acoustic crime of the highest order.

If I were really serious about sound, I would've coated the surfaces of the apartment with a dusting of Italian moss and installed a cork floor. But I'm not that serious.

It's in my nature to question a story the first few times I hear it. The expression "unreliable narrator" is kind of redundant, because narrators are always unreliable. They constantly struggle with their own biases, failing memories, unscientific understandings of the world, narrative interferences from other similar stories, and the distractions of daily life. You can hardly blame anyone for not telling the story straight. That's why I always like to hear it a few times.

Tell me again how you went deaf.

Maybe I should start charging you for this. Especially because it seems to get you off.

Work is work. I'd support that arrangement. Listen, I just want you to tell me again, in case I missed any details the first time around.

I was pretty thorough, if I recall. Remember, I was trying to impress you.

Your memory actually did impress me. But that's not what you were trying to do. You were trying to get my sympathy.

Of course I was, that was the fastest way to bed you.

Did you know that I always knew we would meet? Ever since I was a kid. I'm serious. I imagined you more as a Derek, but you're still pretty much the same guy.

Right.

I have a special narrative request, if you don't mind. Tell me the story from the point of view of the ears.

You're such a psycho.

Our conversations are magical. Stutterer and deaf person, we have such interesting ways of communicating. We meet somewhere in the middle of the other's irregular speech. He lipreads my thoughts through a stutter, and I read his through his slur. When we speak to each other, Eric stares at my mouth, and I stare at his hands. I don't understand sign language so he doesn't sign to me, but his fingers still try to decode what he's saying. He can't help it.

He places his hands on my neck to feel the vibrations. Sometimes I think he knows what I'm going to say a few seconds before it comes out. And sometimes, maybe even before I know what I'm going to say. I place my hands on his sternum, not to feel the vibration, but to feel the pain in his sighs and what happens between words. He's a breathy one. Having a conversation with him engages so much of our bodies. It's so sexual. I think the real reason we talk is to have an excuse to fondle each other. We're real pervs that way. I wonder if I'd love Eric as much if he were a hearing person. And I wonder if he wonders the same about my speech.

Eric the teenager was a suburban brat, a long-haired boy of interesting bone construction. He had a keen social conscience and sense of politics. He was quiet by choice, prematurely aged, and silent beyond his years. This was mostly to boycott the stupidity he saw around him, but also to stoke a smug, adolescent sense of knowing it all. We have all been too smart to interact with the world at some point on our journeys to the centre of the idiot self. He retold his story:

One day, hanging around in the basement with a bunch of other grade-ten intellectuals debating the relevance of Nirvana lyrics, a bug crawled into his ear, or that's how it felt. In response, his face suddenly twitched and jumped. Eric knew enough about bugs to know it wasn't an earwig. There was no wriggling. It was more of a slow, plodding, insistent crawl. He raised his hand to stick his finger in his ear but stopped short. That could just push it in deeper. At his friends' encouragement, he tilted his head, hoping gravity would work. Then he pinched his nose and blew like you do on airplanes, but that didn't work, either. That's when he got more insight into the nature of the bug creeping into him: It had a corpulent, muscled body the shape of a worm, a hard helmet of a head, an antenna that probed and tickled. There may have been wings, because something was opening up. A boy knows when something is unfolding inside him.

What a young know-it-all assumes at this point in the creation of his life story is that the insect was inching its way to the succulent brilliance of his mind, to feed on his brain, lay eggs, suck out his intelligence, shit prolifically into his faculties and lobes, and eventually carry everything out like loot into the bad world.

Eric's friends started to panic because of what was coming out of his mouth. He didn't make any sense; he praised the group Genesis, which, in their social circle, was taboo enough to warrant shunning. They pretended not to hear him say that he wanted to hang a Phil Collins poster over his bed.

For the most part, Eric felt calm. Then he felt the legs under the animal. They were manifold and behaved like hairs. There was something significantly problematic for Eric that an insect inside his ear, a growing itch in his face and head, was covered with legs identical to stereocilia, the "hairs" that made hearing possible. The perfect camouflage. The thoughts raced quickly through Eric's mind, just ahead of the bug. It was planning to domicile itself permanently in his head. It would make a nest of wax and dandruff, absorb sound, become his ear, hear for him. Intercept the signals and rob him of all frequencies.

The insect was no insect, but, rather, an arthropod. It was a millipede. And it was already driving him insane.

Eric panicked and dragged his friends into the car garage adjacent to his bedroom, where they scavenged around for a tool. Nothing looked right to him; everything looked deformed and anthropomorphic, like something from either *Naked Lunch*, *Beauty and the Beast*, or *The Flintstones*, like a roto-rooter with wings, a weedwacker with grass stains on its lips, vise grips in a perpetual metallic death rattle, spools of conductive copper coil hibernating for heat, or nails all fighting loudly for a spot at the bottom of the box.

Suction cup.

The suction cup was just being itself. Eric's dad usually used it to pull dings out of car doors. Eric's friends held his head down against a tire, moved his long hair aside, and affixed the suction cup to his ear. Six hands pressed it flush against him to push all the air out and create a perfect vacuum. One friend grabbed Eric by the neck and held him down while the other two pulled the suction cup up.

When you draw elements through a vacuum, you create an impossibility in space, a zero-gravity situation where blood can free-float, where screams travel but remain silent. The concave part of a suction cup was never meant to contain so much human pain. Eric's head wouldn't fall off the cup. It stayed suspended in mid-air as a set of shears got up and walked out of the garage with a side-winding garden hose. Eric's friends had to mime to him to hold his nose and blow.

Eric didn't hear the rip. His friends did, and they've been trying to describe the sound to him ever since. The bug was never found.

So? Is that different from the first time I told you the story?

It always is. This time you forgot something important. Like reeeeeeeally important.

What?

You want me to tell you?

It sounds like something I should know.

Yes, it's totally something you should know. Maybe I should charge you for it. Story analysts get paid a lot of money.

You're a dick, and I hate and love you at the same time.

You forgot to say what ear it was. And can we assume that there were two millipedes? One for each ear?

I can't believe you. You weren't even listening. You're so busy fucking my lips that you don't spend enough time reading them. That's been the problem ever since we met.

I plunged my tongue into his nearest ear hole without warning, deep-diving into the wax. I skull-fucked him until his earlobes turned a shade of red that matched the sheets. But I was still searching and curious, so I wrapped my tongue around his whole mind, the whole beautiful fucking thing, turning it over in a spit baste, looking for what, I don't know, maybe pricked desire not yet worn sharper by use, or maybe something more liminal, the mud edges of a brain slicked and falling open, as if there could be more, and just before pulling out, I whispered something so that Seal could echo inside him forever unheard, about getting a little crazy just to survive.

PUNISHMENT FOR RECORD THIEVES

There was a time when I needed to listen to every song in the world. I was still looking for the missing parts of me. HMV had a lot of new music, and it had served me well these past few years, but I realized I needed access to older material.

I figured the easiest way to do that was to quit being a bum and volunteer at CKUT FM community radio on rue McTavish. At the time, it housed Canada's largest private record collection. I forget the exact numbers, but they were up there—tens of thousands of vinyl records, CDs, and cassettes, stacked in filing cabinets in the basement of the William Shatner Building at McGill. Musicologists from around the world made pilgrimages to the station. They begged to sleep in the aisles so they could catalogue in dreams as well as in wakefulness, even though that was against the rules.

I would soon become very familiar with the four-letter word, the call letters that the deejays repeated endlessly in gravel voices carved by cigarettes and coffee and long nights during funding drives, on programs that were passed from friend to friend like deathbed heirlooms.

The coordinator squinted at me and frowned when he saw my shoes. They were brand-new.

Do you steal?

Is this what you ask all volunteers?

Yes. We kind of have a problem. A lot of CDs go missing. We don't think it's the volunteers, but we can't be sure. A few hundred pieces of music disappear every year, and we don't know what to do about it.

Only a few hundred?

That's a lot. That's too much.

Have you considered Klingons?

No, we haven't.

I think you should. This is the William Shatner Building.

Just so we're clear, you can't live here. Do you go to McGill?

Uh, no.

Where do you go to school?

Here and there, but not Concordia, so don't worry.

The prospective candidate has to open incoming mail, take out the music, and listen to it on the CD player in the cubicle with the door closed. There's a pair of headphones. You can throw the letter in the garbage.

Do you only get CDs? No cassettes?

Sometimes, but rarely. If you see a cassette, you should notify someone.

What's in the letter?

Nothing, just some garbage from the record label saying we're the first radio station to get the album and that we should be thankful. Just put it in the trash.

What's in the cubicle?

You.

If there are headphones, why does the door have to be closed?

The prospective candidate is doing important and private work. After a first listen, they must label the jewel case with a sticker according to the colour code: green, purple, black, white, orange, pink, magenta.

What about CD covers that are the same colour as the sticker I'm supposed to use? It won't show up.

The prospective candidate should not ask so many questions.

Are you referring to me?

I haven't said whether or not you got the job.

I thought this was a volunteer position. You mean it's a job and there's pay?

Hush up. The prospective candidate, if not sure about the style of music, will listen again. Sometimes there are fine lines. Alternative may not be new wave. Brit pop may not be shoegazer, as vocal jazz may be so far from spoken word that people will question your judgment if you mix them up. Hip hop and dubstep and trip are not the same things. At all.

I know that.

The blue sticker is special. It means the record should go into the MCR, or the Master Control Room. This is music that the volunteer thinks is really, really good and should be played on the air. Like, it does something to you. So when the deejays go into the MCR to prepare their shows, they can check out the new arrivals.

What do you mean "does something" to me?

You'll know.

Can I go on the air?

The prospective candidate may not speak on the radio. The volunteer is in charge of processing the CDs and putting them in the right stacks, alphabetically and based on the stickers. The volunteer may not smoke in the cubicle.

Am I the volunteer?

The prospective candidate is the volunteer. The volunteer must burn the call letters C-K-U-T into the inner plastic ring of every CD, careful not to damage the music. This is done with a soldering iron.

No one told me about this.

I'm telling you now. This is a key part of the job. It discourages theft. The volunteer can put the wrong sticker on the jewel case. It happens and the CD will be misplaced, but it's not that bad. At least the CD will still be in the building. But if it's not engraved, it will go missing. That's worse.

Why is that a deterrent? What thief would care?

The thief will have a harder time selling the CD. The prospective candidate should not be the thief.

I'm not … So, am I the prospective candidate?

No. You are the volunteer. Congratulations.

I installed myself in a cubicle the size of a phone booth, windowless and beige, barely enough room for the table and chair. I looked at the stack of envelopes, and it made me think of my old band. I felt a twinge of sadness that we never got to mail in our stuff, that it was absent from the pile and always would be.

I opened the first envelope. It was from PolyGram Music Canada. I threw the letter in the garbage without reading it and tore the shrink wrap off the CD case. It was a single. "Regret" by New Order. I couldn't believe it. I was still trying to fill the emotional hole that Ian Curtis had left in me by committing suicide. Strange that I had that hole, even though he'd died when I was a toddler. But we are all free to grieve whomever we want, and to choose our own fairy dogparents.

I figured I'd give the CD a generous ten seconds. I stuck it in, pressed play, and something weird happened. Bernard Sumner's opening chords hung in midair above me in the cubicle. Like an aura, a holy apparition, a fart. I didn't know songs could be holographic, but this one seemed to have a three-dimensional presence. The song poured out of the headphones and into the room. Thirty seconds in, and I was Peter Hooked. Sumner sang about forgetting the name and the address of everyone he'd ever known. Was that even possible? The idea was so fresh to me, it made me light-headed. It was exactly what I needed to do at that time in my life: retreat from everybody so I could figure things out. Disappear. And this was the place to do it. I played the song twenty or thirty times and had a long cry, a head rush that turned from migraine to endorphin depth charge from one bar to the next, a nervous breakdown and consequent reassembly, hallucinations, visions of god that made me ask, if Ian Curtis had figured out a way to disappear among the living, would he still have killed himself? It took me another few listens to realize he would've done it anyway.

Sumner sang about strangers in a way that made me understand how familiar they were and always would be. In the end, there was no need to worry about losing someone's phone number. There was always another way to find them.

"Regret" turned out to be the song that defined my summer. I was barely a teenager anymore, so it was uncouth to have single songs that changed everything, but fuck it. I reserved the right to prolong teenagehood, and so developed my love affair with the cubicle and its swirling claustrophobic madness, but also my intense disappointment with every envelope that followed, because it wasn't New Order. I would never again hear bass so resonant that it shook everything I believed in.

It was only my first day on the job, and the best was already over.

I gave the CD a blue sticker.

It just so happens that most of my musical research centres on letters of the alphabet I can't pronounce. I swear, it's a coincidence. When you're looking for a specific song you think was the soundtrack to a significant moment in your life, you have to be thorough.

Brought to you by the letter C:

Creedence Clearwater Revival, the Clash, Corgan and the rest of the Pumpkins, all of them smashing, Callas peaking at l'Arc du Triomphe, the Commodores and the Vegas bootlegs, the Carpenters who taught me that Mondays were good for nothing (Karen still has to sing me through them), Johnny Cash and Patsy Cline mysteriously never on the same side of the AM dial, Costello, "Come to My Window," cassettes on the verge of extinction, Crystal Waters was never homeless, cymbals, call and response, we all know that Marilyn Manson's "Cake and Sodomy" and Elton John's *Captain Fantastic and the Brown Dirt Cowboy* are about the same thing, Cab

Calloway, "Camptown Races."

The volunteer coordinator was right about the thief problem. We had an infestation. I could detect the presence of burglars even when I was locked in my cubicle and wearing headphones. That's how sensitive I was. I caught them crawling through the window, using empty loot bags to protect themselves against the broken glass and then cushion their falls. Some of them pretended to be janitors or journalists or movers or even volunteers, and dared to walk straight through the front door. One dude had the nerve to say his volunteer job was to replace old records with new ones.

They knew I could see right through their excuses, so most of them didn't even bother. After capture, their fear was palpable. We were alone in a basement. Maybe they could sense that I took the break-ins personally, that I was indignant with them.

The truth was that I wanted the music all to myself.

Punishments: The first round was always a solid mugging. I'd handcuff them to the radiator and raid their pockets for bills and change. I wouldn't know what to do with credit cards, so I left those. And I took their Discmans because they contained a substance that I needed. I think this kind of counter-robbery fucked with my head as much as it did theirs. They knew something much worse was coming, and I confirmed that suspicion by plugging in the soldering iron. When an animal is locked in a pen, that's the perfect time to brand it. I got creative and chose different punishments:

Some days, on the arm, the back of the hand, or the upper inner thigh, depending what they wore and where it would be visible, and where I thought it would hurt the most.

Some days, I engraved into the flesh of these screaming, begging criminals the names of the artists they were trying to steal. It was particularly unfortunate for the detainee when it was a long name or an artist formerly known as something else, and out of fairness, I had to inscribe both names.

Some days, I tried to carve a facsimile of the album cover, at least *les grandes lignes* with a reasonable amount of shading. Of course, this required a good stretch of uninterrupted dermal real estate.

Some days, I engraved the time and date when I apprehended them.

Some days, I administered anaesthetic in the form of gin and tonic made with premium Hendrick's, cucumber, a dash of muddled blueberries, rubbing alcohol, and unleaded gasoline. Other days, I wanted them to feel more, to be truly present in the moment that was marking us both.

Some days, I made them watch the searing, the smoke of flesh. Other days, I blindfolded them and made them listen to it.

Some days, I was a fickle bastard and couldn't decide what technique was best, so I did all of them. So very me.

Most days, I was jealous of their punishment.

You'd think that the most logical thing was to solder C-K-U-T into these burglars, but it never occurred to me. It did strike me, however, to burn my name into every single one of them. My station now, my name always.

Brought to you by the letter H:

"Hey Yew Gotta Loight Boy" by the Singing Postman, Heart, Hammond B3s and other organs, hitting the high-hat a second too soon, Hole, "Hello, It's Me," John Helliwell without the rest of Supertramp, hipster warblings, Happy Mondays before ecstasy tabs melted through their guitar tabs, Harry Belafonte, "Horse with No Name," hinting out of habit that this is the final show, heroin parties with Lou Reed, helicons and hurdy-gurdies, hammers on harpsichord strings, Harmonium, hemp T-shirts at the merch table, Hammerstein & Rogers, tell me that it's "Human Nature," "Hangin' Tough" with the New Kids, "High School Confidential" (although "Hickory Dickory Dock" was more my speed), the Hornbostel-Sachs categories of sound-producing material including directly struck idiophones, Max Headroom stuttering through a Pepsi commercial.

PENISES I HAVE LOVED AND NOT LOVED

Sometimes I think that if I stare at enough cocks, cocks of all shapes and colouring, of varied ridge and vein formations, degrees of smell, shades of blond and brown and red in the pubic hair, protrusions and protuberances in slightly different directions, angles of piss never a certain gamble, that I will think, *Hey, I have never seen this one before*, the drooping foreskin, the skyward curvature; some penises take a greater or lesser interest in me, some of them inch over one at a time or keep an impressively measured distance, diffident to my glances, standoffish in a pocket of underwear, breaching through fabric here and there, curled and sleeping in a soft pouch, grossly indecent and outright puritanical, penises that have been abused by the rigours of soap and kept too clean, unsuitable for fucking but perfect for church; I stare from all angles and try to recognize a penis I have seen before, the ones that have stared me down, sidled over to cross swords, dripped hungrily onto my nose, anointed me on the forehead, sniffed out my bum, bouncing and glistening with pre-cum, either blithe or over-aware of my presence, a shaft that never worked out its kinks, I'll say, *Hey, a certain softness seems familiar to me*, scrotal sweat moist and rank, droplets following the path of least resistance and onto my face; I am always the path of least resistance for some reason, reptilian skin constantly shifting with the temperature of my breath, testicles that are evenly weighted with the exception of pea-shaped cancerous lumps, sebaceous cysts that stare at me like eyes, pubic hair shaved into a baseball diamond, into a runaway runway strip like at Mirabel Airport, plumpers never fully hard, I'll say, *Hey, how could I have measured size back when I was growing at least half a foot a year*, discharge in crayon colours, a mushroom head that swells in my mouth until it cuts off airflow.

I figure if I steal a glance at every penis that takes a piss beside me, I'll eventually see the one this is all about, the first one, unless the first one was mine.

SPEECH THERAPY FOR THE BENT

Our cart was full even before we got to the second aisle. That's how it goes at the supermarket with Eric and me. He comes with a list balanced on the four food groups, taking into account the room in the fridge and the room in the cupboard, our impossibly small freezer, careful not to overbuy, and aware that things go rotten. For me, the supermarket is like a candy store or a bar, or like sex—I don't want to have to hold back on anything. That would feel counterintuitive to the shopping experience.

I'm not going to discuss the number of hard-ons I've had over the years as I've pushed the squeaky cart down the aisle, considering the implications: it's the ultimate capitalist orgy where nothing is lacking, where overabundance conceals want, where denial is sold in bulk. Consumer excess in all its gaudy glory. Maybe I'm addicted to the guilt. We all have our things. It's difficult for me to describe my love for the supermarket without getting emotional. The cereal aisle—I pass through it like it's a parted Red Sea and weep over the breakfast possibilities.

You're not supposed to get off on capitalism, but I can't help it.

However, this is only when I'm alone. When I'm with Eric, I behave somewhat. He is my electrical ground. I simply and calmly throw more things in the cart than are on our agreed-upon list and hope he doesn't notice. When I participate in the creation of the list, it's a falsity because I don't reveal my full consumer desires or the extent of my enslavement to them. Anyway, how do you know when your boyfriend knows your true preferences? Was eighteen months enough time together for him to have figured it out?

I attempted to turn our cart down the dairy aisle, and Eric questioned the move.

We have enough milk.

I think we're low on cheese.

We have enough cheese.

Then margarine. Ours has too many toast crumbs in it.

Eric let us proceed. Toad the Wet Sprocket was playing over the sound system. Then he did something I didn't expect. He picked up three cans of whipped cream and put them in the cart. I stared at the hole they left on the shelf. He was spoiling me. Showing off. I was so turned on.

Eric preferred to start at the back of the supermarket so that we ended up in fresh fruit. That way, the fruit sits on top and doesn't get crushed. I think there's something inherently flawed with that system. In my opinion, it would make more sense to end up in frozen, so that our cold purchases would keep the whole cart chilled. A small but important difference of opinion.

This was as good a place as any to ask him.

I need us to try a new kind of sex.

We should get some onions.

Eric picked up a bag of white onions, two pounds, and then a lone red Spanish onion, which he weighed on the scale to determine the price. He squeezed a spaghetti squash for readiness, even though gourds are always hard, so I knew he was distracted. I had thrown him off with my question. I tapped him to make him look at my mouth again.

What do you think about what I just asked you?

I suppose I'll need to know more.

There are some things we can do in bed that would be, um, good for me.

Okay.

I feel bad for saying this, but it's also something I need to experience alone. You know? Like, yeah. It's kind of private. But—

So do you want to be alone, or do you want to have sex with me? Which is it?

That's the thing. It's both. I need to be alone sometimes while we're having sex.

You don't have enough privacy when we fuck?

He stares at my lips when I speak, especially when it's something he doesn't want to miss. This time, he was forced to watch, by virtue of the circumstances, a particularly rabid display of saliva, because I had stolen a cherry and once again decided to test my allergy to stone fruits. By then, I had stopped caring about reactions, the inevitable puffy lips and closing of the throat.

No, that's not it.

You need me to leave the room so you don't have performance anxiety about getting hard?

Thanks for bringing that up.

Babe, I'm just asking for information. Sorry.

That's okay.

Well, tell me what this means for me in practical terms.

Um, it could mean that I don't explain why I'm asking you to do certain things to me when we're in bed?

Of course. That's understood. I never ask too many questions of you.

I know. I wasn't saying that.

Why do you always get so weird when we do groceries?

Eric headed for the self-checkout machines, and I started to get nauseated. That was the perfect way to ruin a shopping trip: a desultory passing of items in front of a laser. It made me sick. I would much rather have been at the human checkout a few feet over, where our mountain of purchases could be inspected, reviled, and envied by the voyeurs in line behind us. The cashier would touch every single item with their hands, feel every single perverted and irresponsible decision we made that day; the obscenely wasteful packaging, the toxic ingredients shaming us, delivering humiliation by turning the items over and over, looking for the bar codes. Then asking if we wanted paper bags, as if our purchases must be hidden. But those are just my preferences. Every experience is a sexual one for me.

Back at home, we put the groceries away together in silence. There were limbo items, the ones that could go either in the fridge or the pantry. We took our time deciding. I was happy with the day's shopping because our fridge was getting full. A full fridge can compensate for a lot of things: deficiencies, holes, hungers. New jars and cans of stuff hide the half-full and half-eaten. Sometimes I buy something I already have. Not sometimes. All the time.

We made dinner together. Eric peeled the carrots meticulously. He threw half the peels into the garbage and ate the rest. I worked on the potatoes. Washing, peeling, boiling, mashing. I was annoyed when the potatoes boiled over and the scummy water dried on the stovetop. I prepared the dinner table with plates and cutlery and poured us some drinks. We waited for dinner to be ready. I think we were both busy imagining what was going to happen in bed. I had a pretty clear picture, but I wondered about not feeling anything. Sometimes not even a wild fantasy can give you what you're looking for, especially if you're looking for something buried in time.

I can never get enough of Eric's smell. That's why I toss and turn so much, in a mad sleepy dash to get as much of his fresh night scent as I can. I always wake up jet-lagged and on the other side of the bed. I'm convinced that I float through the thick substance of him somewhere in a dream world, that his body is a kind of semiconductor. That's when I'm open to Eric. Other nights, I seem to be closed off; we are two sarcophagi who don't interact, our broken embraces a numb truth that hangs in the air as we lie awake and wonder how many hours until we roll away from each other into another morning both together and apart. The consistency of my spirit isn't made for this madness.

We both need to cum in the morning. I know we should conserve the day's energy for partying and socializing and activism, but fuck it, we're slaves to orgasm, and we both serve as terrible reminders of that fact to each other. I was ready to try my sex game. It's the epitome of disempowerment. I wondered what my activist friends would think.

That morning, the sun was streaming through cracks in the blinds. It cut across our limbs and caught the blond fur on his legs.

Let's do it.

Okay, maybe.

I'll need more than a maybe.

Do I have to wear anything?

No, you actually have to wear nothing.

Then what do I have to do?

Why do you automatically assume submission?

Is submission involved?

Yes. But I'll be the one submitting.

But if this is your game and you're telling me what to do, doesn't that make you dominant?

Oh my god, do we have to be such basic queers? Can we step it up?

Okay, tell me about it and I'll consider.

You'll be face fucking me, and I'll be resisting you.

That sounds pretty vanilla. What framework will we have in place for continued consent?

Don't ruin this for me.

I'm just being responsible.

I handed Eric a stack of numbered cue cards. For dramatic inspiration, I wrote them while watching *General Hospital*, my favourite soap opera. I watched it with the sound muted and put words in the mouths of the actors. The character arcs would never be the same, not after what I made them say to each other. Eric appeared troubled as he flipped through the stack. He started shaking his foot, a nervous tic that rarely manifested.

I don't want to be responsible for damaging you.

You won't. This is my idea.

I still want you to have safe words for different levels of escalation, especially considering where you're taking this.

We can stop if it gets too heavy for you.

Eric sighed and closed his eyes, perhaps to get into character. Then he opened them and read the first cue card.

Say my name.

It gave me an instant erection. Not bad for a guy with an early case of erectile dysfunction. I turned bright red and got very hot and shy. This was an immaculate transfusion of devil's blood.

Say my name. I said, say my fucking name.

Eh-eh-eh-

Say it.

Eh-eh-eh-

Swallow, choke, vacillate, my entire world a hesitation. His aggression made it impossible to close my mouth to enunciate the letter R.

Say it.

Eh-eh-eh

He slid himself higher in juxtaposition to me on the bed.

Say my name, you stuttering freak, you deformity of nature.

I started to pre-cum hard, a stream of semen unspooling from the top of my dick into a growing dark spot on the sheet. Like when I pissed the bed as a little boy, I couldn't hide my humiliation.

Eh-eh-eh

I've said his name perfectly thousands of times, but in this situation, I was powerless. For a stutterer, there is no safe word, because there is no guarantee you'll be able to say it.

Eh-eh-r-eh

I couldn't get my top teeth to touch my bottom lip long enough to form the letter. My jaws felt like the north poles of two magnets being held against each other.

Can't say it? I didn't think so.

He moved up the bed, grabbed me by the hair, and yanked my face closer to him. My head jerked and spasmed. I tried to say his name, a simple two syllables any idiot could manage, any idiot but me.

The reason you can't close your mouth is because you're waiting for me to shove my dick inside. You want me to face-fuck the stutter right out of you.

He pushed his crotch closer. I shook my head "no" as my nose filled with the smell of his big sweaty balls, dangling in my face. I tried to push him away, but he restrained my hands under his knees and sat on my chest. I made one last effort to say his name and avoid the inevitable. I took a deep breath and tried again.

Eh-eh-eh-eh-Eh-r-eh

He shoved his fat uncut cock right into the space of his half-uttered name and pushed himself down my throat until I gagged and almost puked. I tried to buck him off me, but he was too heavy.

Fucking look at me. I'm the word you are trying to say, and now the word is coming to choke you.

He pumped my face silly until tears streamed down my cheeks. I looked up at him in fear and terror and love. Perhaps as a reprieve, Eric pulled his dick out of my face to give me one last chance.

Eric.

I did it. Flawlessly. But he closed his eyes just as I said it, so he didn't see. An aspect of the game I hadn't considered.

He stuck his cock back inside me to make up for my deficiency, to correct it. By then, I had surrendered to him. He expanded in my throat. At our age, in our early twenties, less than five decades combined and already jaded, this was hardly enough to make either of us cum, so he used his speaking privilege to deliver the final blow, his *coup de petit mort*, and it was ruthless and brilliant on my back molars and in my spinning, exploding head. He enunciated better than any actor I had ever seen on *General Hospital*.

You're just a little boy who has never learned how to speak.

Those words. My orgasm was a series of tiny moments, finite particles accelerating to an infinite crash: Eric suddenly pulled out, and through his legs I saw my foreskin sleeked back in my hand; I was a kid again, with a boner so hard it wouldn't bend, squeezing knuckle white, squeezing knuckle red, fingers coated in the first dribble of sperm lava, no pubes in sight because they were hidden (unless they had fallen out in the shiver of fantasy) squeezing knuckle red, squeezing knuckle blue, fingering my tight boy ass and wondering how much it could take. When had I first imagined anything so elaborate and exquisite and sinister? I just started to laugh, because my dick poked through my Donald Duck boxers where Donald's beak hole would be, so both Eric and I were, in fact, face-raping a stutterer.

I laughed and laughed and sprayed the bed with hot cum until I was empty of mind and spirit. Empty in reams. Empty of dreams. Thunder doesn't only happen when it's raining. You can be draining, too.

He got off me and I collapsed into his arms, exhausted, happy, and full of wonder about the world and my place in it. He seemed remote. Are you okay?

Yes.

Why didn't you cum?

This was about you.

Did you like it?

It was good.

Just good?

You're being insecure. I would like you to be more secure in the cruelty you inflict on yourself.

We each retreated to our side of the bed. I felt like telling him that there can be no regret for a perfect orgasm, no matter what it takes to get there. That, like modernist art, it needs no justification. That fantasy cannot crumble our belief systems. But he was already engrossed in a book, and soon I was too. I wondered if we were both reading aimlessly while our brains worked out the question of whether or not we were bad people.

I wondered what it would be like to do what he did to someone else.

SCREAMING HANDFUL OF NOTHING

For some reason, I started to panic that I wouldn't find the music I was looking for at CKUT. Radio stations could be tune cemeteries, for all I knew, where pop hits went to gentrify and die. Maybe the answers were lurking in random Walkmans and Discmans around the city, in the secrets that people played to themselves as they caromed around and avoided each other. I decided to put my theory to the test.

I found myself in the Place-des-Arts Metro station one day, staring at people more than I usually do. There was a twenty-something guy with cornrows and a beard and a really creative way of twisting a scarf through his hair so it looked feathered. His clothes were filled with mysterious pockets. I eventually landed on his eyes, and we locked. I held them across the platform and pulled him several feet before finally letting go. Then there was the person in the clothes of the. preppy young professional—pinstripe suit, crisp and starched white dress shirt, canary-yellow hankie—obviously so many secrets to hide under all those codes. Made me curious. But soon I was distracted by a new round of passengers who had just descended into the station: Woman in punk T-shirt, baby punks in big punk clothing, day jobbers and people coming home from all-nighters. They collectively turned into a grey sludge of humanity, a mass of meat run through a sluice and decayed to the colour of rotting flesh and maggots. I wanted to know what music they listened to, what had made them that way. Perhaps I craved their boredom.

Their eyes were like mine, empty mirrors, reflecting pools with holes in them, searching for a missing piece of themselves in another, endlessly darting from face to face, as I was doing, looking for a spot of recognition in the light of another, a place of relief to rest temporarily, take a break from the search. All eyes travelling and revealing nothing. Birds over the ocean with nothing to do but keep flying.

I started to notice the people wearing headphones. They were different, their eyes free of armour. There was honesty in the waves of their movements. It connected in my head like a line of dots, like little blue stickers.

I knew that the only way to honesty, to the truth, was to rip the headphones off every music listener I passed in the hopes of finding out what made them so peaceful and remote, not necessarily in contrast with the others on the platform, but rather, in contrast with me. I did it one by one, swiped their headphones in swift moves, knocking off hats and sunglasses, completely destabilizing them while they tottered at the edge of the platform as a train approached.

I lifted the jangle of headphones up to my head, a multi-headed hydra hissing treble and screaming mid-range. I listened intently but heard nothing that I was seeking in this cacophony.

Trouble is, I couldn't shake the wires. I ran off the platform and up the stairs dragging all this music behind me, with angry people trying to grab me by the strings.

BROUGHT TO YOU BY THE LETTER M

There is a slew of things I want Eric to hear, and it upsets me that he can't. So I just keep lists of them and randomly Hotmail them to him, hoping the imagined sounds burst the hidden eardrums in his head:

Machine-gunning through broken concepts that are otherwise smooth, murderous attacks on consonants, murmuring to make the listener think the problem is their hearing and not my speech, mixing metaphors if the conflict will be less than a mouthful, meandering from the subject, mmmmm sounds that lead people to believe I find daily existence more delicious than it actually is, marbles tumbling in the space a name should occupy, milking the first half of a word, hoping the last half changes shape before coming out, mangling a thought to the point where someone questions my sureness or my honesty, mouthing things to myself seconds before I say them, missed practice runs, mistaken signs of affection, Morrissey, Mike + the Mechanics, Massive Attack, Maori singers, *mamase mamasa mamacusa.*

Mostly, I want him to hear that I speak everything voiced to him, when all he needs is to see my mouth.

I want him to know that I stutter for him even though I don't have to.

IN THE LIONS' DEN

When I think back to the Jehovah's Witness literature I used to "read," there were some pretty hot illustrations of Daniel in the Lions' Den.

If I have to analyze how I really feel about the story, I'd have to say it's completely overblown and far too allegorical. The prophets were deluded and wrote their spurious scriptures while high on lead poisoning, so you can't really blame Daniel.

After discarding a theory I once considered—that the lions' mouths weren't actually sealed, but rather, the lions were simply afraid of stuttering and showing weakness—I concluded that it is actually the story of a prisoner and his captor.

It was a prison of the Biblical variety, but modern with wrought-iron bars and locks. The same kind of prison exists all over the world today. The formula caught on. It doesn't matter what the prison looked like. But let's say the walls were covered with insanities, etchings of the minds of the obscene, prisoners gone mad with the imperceptible passage of time. It doesn't matter if there was one prisoner or there were many; they would all experience pain to the same extremity and lose themselves in one another. They would try to murder each other, thinking it was suicide.

The captor never spoke.

One day, a prisoner convinced himself that the captor was there to hear his confession. Perhaps there was something in the quality of the captor's silence that made him think that. Something patient. Something receptive.

So the prisoner unburdened himself.

"This is my confession. I have lied in the eyes of the Lord for unjust gain. My neighbour undertook to purchase an ass from me, and I misrepresented the health of the animal. The ass was indeed quite lame, but I exacted a premium price for it. The animal died the day after purchase, and I went to bed laughing at the misfortune and stupidity of my neighbour. I have every right to be in this cell."

The captor still didn't speak. He sat on a wooden chair in the heat, scraping the resin off the chair's back leg with a knife. He smeared it on a tiny piece of dry bread and ate it. He stared at the wall with no facial expression that the prisoner could recognize.

The prisoner assumed that the captor was dissatisfied with what he'd said, that perhaps he hadn't been forthcoming or contrite enough. Because the captor was silent, the prisoner didn't know what else to do except fill the air with words.

"This is my confession. I have lied in the eyes of the Lord for unjust gain, but not completely how I just told you. The animal got well again and became one of the strongest working asses. It took load after load without a complaint, and allowed its body to be broken under the weight of barley and millet. In the hot sun, it refused to drink water lest it be considered a lazy and selfish beast. The weight of the produce of the earth carved into the animal muscles of marble, and its work reaped many spoils for my neighbour. I grew jealous of this, of how the animal worked harder for my neighbour than for me. So I poisoned the animal in the night, and then, when the neighbour mourned over the corpse, I came behind him and slit his throat, and I took back my money."

Still he didn't speak, the captor.

It is not part of this story to explain if God sealed the captor's mouth, or if Satan did it. And I don't know what effect wood resin has on human lips.

The captor played with the key to the jail-cell lock. He bent down to dig a keyhole into the dirt floor. He scraped and scraped and jammed the key into the ground. The captor created a lock that wouldn't turn. Just for fun. This drove the prisoner resolutely mental. It snapped something deep in his cerebellum, releasing a poison into his brain. It was the poison of words he had never heard himself think before. The prisoner filled the air with them. It didn't matter what they were or if they were true. He just filled the void because he had to speak for both of them.

"In my lifetime, I have drilled holes into boats on my birthdays so I could watch them sink and the sailors perish at the precise moment I turned another year older. I have baked bread using glass powder and served it to royalty to see if their insides disintegrated at the same speed as those of common folk and if their vomiting of blood was as pedestrian. I have defiled whole herds of swine in the rectum, held a prophet at knifepoint and forced him to write scripture in which he cast me as a saint. I have eaten cloven-hoofed animals on the holiest of days and proclaimed Beelzebub to be my Holy Father. I have shown up in court numerous times, at random trials of accused I did not know, to provide the false evidence the executioner needed to hang them, merely so I could witness the spontaneous erections of other men while they strangled—as a form of personal pornography."

The prisoner, utterly exhausted from his performance, began to shake and fell violently upon the ground. Did he think his confession would earn him quicker release, a fuller pardon? Does honesty breed sympathy?

He said nothing, the captor.

The prisoner—about to lose consciousness, feeling close to death, certain that all his organs would fail at any minute now that he had emptied himself of every criminal possibility true and untrue, feasible and unfeasible, damnable and undamnable—stared at the keyhole the captor had dug into the dirt floor. He then began to wonder: If the floor was made of dirt, why hadn't he thought of digging himself out?

"I didn't do any of it."

The captor finally spoke.

"I know. And that is why you are here. We are in the business of imprisoning innocent people."

COPROFAGIA

I was once again stuck in a capitalist wet dream with a boyfriend who wasn't remotely interested.

He's the better lover by a long shot. He's less abrasive, less presumptuous, kinder, more thoughtful, more responsible, more forgiving. He holds the threads of a relationship more delicately. He's good at spotting moments better shared than experienced alone. The best, embarrassingly so.

But he is absolutely terrible at buying furniture we don't need. I, on the other hand, excel in that area of wastefulness.

I was still apologizing to Eric for having tried to push him toward hearing restoration surgery when he didn't want it. I had even booked a consultation without telling him, and it turned out to be the worst birthday present I ever gave anyone. I had been in damage-control mode ever since, but I was afraid that my overtures were falling on, ahem, deaf ears. So I tried other ways of showing him that I was sorry. In a bid to give us a fresh start, I had proposed that we ditch all of our furniture and start over, reupholster our lives anew. We were adults but would soon be grown-ups. He gingerly agreed to a few new pieces.

I was grateful for this opening and showed him the items I had already circled in the IKEA catalogue: the shower curtains with hologram inlay of downtown Stockholm; white Pappasan chair with red circular bull's-eye stitching; dining room table with bevelled glass and chrome legs; inverse bookshelf that defied gravity and looked like an upside-down Machu Picchu. These were the manifestations of my love—collapsible, available, on sale, and easy to put together. Everything was tasteful, in my opinion, but Eric wrinkled his nose. I suggested we go there in person to see the furniture up close. He relented to a ninety-minute in-store visit. I ushered him out the door and told him to say goodbye to our old life.

We took the bus to IKEA, and I directed us to a thoroughly greasy, disgusting, but affordable breakfast of industrial scrambled eggs and sausage links in the cafeteria before we proceeded to the actual shopping.

Didn't your mother used to come here a lot?

Why do you always have to bring up my mother?

Uh, I hardly ever. And that's because this is the reaction you always give me. Since we can't talk about your mother, I don't talk about mine. We're completely motherless because of you.

That's not true.

Yes, it is. Your silence around her is really creepy.

Can we not talk about this right now? You're harshing my buzz.

Most shoppers browse the showroom where everything is put together, but I prefer to stroll through the warehouse aisles, the domain of forklifts, uninteresting to the typical shopper unless you happen to get off on reading, on the sides of boxes, in no less than eight languages, warning labels, the quantity of bolts in each length and calibre, how many dowels and tools are required, the number of Allen keys included, and persons needed for setup. I'm a hopeless foamer for instructional detail. People like me keep every IKEA Allen key they've ever used, even though they're identical and all you need is one. Eric appears to put up with it.

I'd like us to try a new kind of sex.

We already did.

I mean another kind. There can be a few different kinds of sex.

Sure thing, mister dickly. Is it something K-9 this time?

No—there. There's the sofa we wanted.

That takes up too much space.

Read my lips. We have the space. I'm going to throw everything out tomorrow.

I think you have a problem. You have an addiction.

You should be more careful when throwing around words like that. Whether or not I have a problem is for me to decide, and me alone.

When will you learn to trust me? I don't know why I agreed to this psychotic trip.

You didn't agree. I forced you. Listen, there's something I've always wanted to try in bed. Like, I *need* it or something? Who knows. The logistics might be hard to figure out. Then there's the matter of our feelings. That's another thing entirely. Oh boy, here's a futon with rubber wheels for front legs. Easy to move around.

What is it?

I was wondering … how you feel about scat.

Uh…

I just want to say that you're not under any pressure or anything. But it's something I need to do. It might be a way of regressing for me, getting to the root of things. I don't know. It's about being primal. Letting my body be as messy as my emotions. Getting to the insides of me that I don't understand.

The way you intellectualize sex is unsexy. Can't it be as simple as you just liking shit?

Ha. Hadn't thought of that.

And you're saying that you want to get shit all over our brand-new furniture? In that case, I suggest we get everything in shit brown.

You're taking this remarkably well, I think.

Why don't you post an ad in the back of those sex magazines you read? You'll probably have better luck there than with me.

If I write an ad for this and you see it, is there a chance you'll respond?

Yes, if I need to send you spelling corrections.

It bugs me that the artist renderings of the different pieces of furniture, in black ink on the brown cardboard boxes, is such a blatant victim of two-dimensional printing. So many things can throw the shopper's impression askew, including creases in the cardboard, printing density, gaps in the ink, lighting and glare, the distraction of so many wonderful things, the design of the product conflicting with the design of the packaging. They could easily include a hologram of the item, or even a 3-D cardboard cut-out. These ideas of mine have to be remotely Swedish; they can't be completely crazy.

The only thing we ended up buying that day was a doormat,

because it was the only thing we could agree on.

I wasn't exactly sure why I wanted to get into scat. I don't know if I believed the reasons I gave Eric. I think I *did* need to explore it from a somewhat intellectual point of view, so the ad I submitted was longer than I expected. I was sure there was someone out there who had already felt this way but had suppressed, sublimated, ignored, and ultimately, punished themselves for their ideas. So I was hopeful about finding someone into this stuff.

I forget exactly how the ad went, but it included my idea that the perfect song had ten assholes taking a shit on a set of cymbals; how I'd heard a rumour that Edith Piaf was buried with a shit inside her, and exhuming her would release an extinct form of sadness into the world, a single endless note of agony; rumours that toilet paper is the gentrification of shit; that nobody ever leaves a floater by accident; that Georges Bataille was a compulsive wiper; that shit made of silicone is actually just a dildo falling out; that diaper lovers are mystics; that in scat there is no top and bottom, only jazz, and everyone submits; that two people can never shit at precisely the same time, two rosebuds blooming side-by-side but out of synch, not hopeless just tragically usual; that maybe, if we try hard, terrestrially speaking, to understand the love that sits heavy in our bowels, if we finally understand that we can never love another shit more than our own, that all this time we have only ever wanted to shit into our own mouths while saying something important, words choked and forced back inside; that the fear of shit is an enemy, a policing, so when someone says, "that's shitty," "this smells like shit," "hey shit for brains," "hey asshole," or "don't be a shitty-shit shit head," I'll either assume they work for the Conservative Party of Canada and are trying to kill my orgasm, or I'll wonder why they are showering compliments and trying to turn me on; I wrote something about finger fucking myself over a sewer to deform a perfect shape, dreaming of shit that comes out in the shape of its shitter, pinching my nose to hold the smell in, shooting down drones that spy on the shit of the innocent, blowing an armada of suppositories into another endless someone, reading sphincter folds like tea leaves, interpreting regularity as a form of fluency (and therefore a myth), busting nozzles on cans of air freshener, enlisting a heart as a Trojan horse to the ass, and sewing a transnational flag for the shit sniffers and fart fuckers of the world.

I didn't get any responses, but I'm not surprised. I didn't actually say what I wanted to do, and I forgot to put in my Hotmail address.

THE MEAT OF IT

My bed became an operating table. The king-sized silk sheets became a starched white single that smelled of bleach. The walls were cool white and green, the furniture gone and replaced with expensive medical equipment—X-ray machines, defibrillators, heart monitors, ventilators. There were tubes and syringes and cotton swabs on a tray where the night table used to be. A tinted observation window where the sun used to be. Four faceless surgeons, a hospital gown where I used to be naked, no more pillows but my head propped up on a neck stirrup, padded at the side so I couldn't hear well, and a curtain raised in front of my nose so I couldn't see what was happening to my mouth.

They gave me a local anaesthetic, a giant needle that stuck me deep in the throat. I could feel the numbness creep in, the gap in the synaptic messages. I wasn't sure if the doctors realized this, but I could see everything in the glare of the plastic panes on the overhead lamp. My mouth was stretched open with forceps like I was going to give birth to something through my face.

I could feel that something was fucked. And that's when I knew they were out to completely destroy my voice. They were going to rip my larynx open, scalpel right to the heart of it, peel back the skin and tissue like it was an artichoke, find the meat of my stutter, and examine it trembling under the hot white light, the insides of my throat writhing in a pool of blood in their hands. It was a cold study—maybe there was a "cure" or maybe there was nothing they could do—they just had to excise it and toss it into the medical waste, the mechanisms of my voice box open and laid out. There were definitely no safe words. A voice can't make sound when it's so exposed to the elements, it can only vibrate uselessly, and maybe, just maybe, if the light caught it right, the doctors would be able to make out an intention, a wish, a regret, an expression of love, an exasperated rasp, a pleasure growl, choked laughter, reduced to its zero-sum parts. There might still be something to analyze, so the head surgeon took another slice.

The decision had been made long before I got to the operating room: My voice was going to be removed. With my mouth agape at the ceiling, the anaesthesia mask descending over my nose, the gas turned on, the suction turned on, the saw turning, there was nothing to do but close my eyes.

But it turned out to be worse than I had imagined.

In the dream, the doctors turned me into a non-stutterer. It ruined my life. Because now that the stutter had been excised, the continued interruptions could only be explained by one thing: I willfully refused to say what was on my mind.

In subsequent dreams, I took them to court. My lawyer was the Grand Antonio, and he beat them silly with a hunk of mortadella until they confessed to malpractice, and then he ate them.

PRESENTÉ PAR LA LETTRE E

En Vogue, les Everly Brothers, Electric Light Orchestra, Everclear, le début de la chanson "The End" par the Doors, enregistrements perdus et retrouvés dans la glace, Engelbert Humperdinck, les énoncés contre la guerre, Everything But the Girl, les folies électro-acoustiques, "Every Day I Get the Blues" (pas juste toi, Gerry Boulet), erreurs de synchronisation entre la contrebasse et la batterie, "Et si tu n'existais pas," Enigma, entretiens avec Enya dans lesquels elle dénonce la musique d'Enigma en tant que plagiat, Eno et l'évolution de la musique actuelle, "Échappé belle" de Beau Dommage, Ella Fitzgerald, l'ergonomie de l'oreille, Elvis Presley, émetteurs de fréquences extra-terrestres, ex-membres qui nous manquent, Eric's Trip, "l'Exile" de Harmonium, "Elle a fait un bébé toute seule."

BROKEN PEOPLE

Sometimes Eric likes to try to talk me out of ideas. He rarely succeeds, but I appreciate the effort he puts into it. Especially because I know the reason he tries so hard is love.

He claims to be able to see danger long before I can. An extra sense, perhaps, that he developed to make up for deafness. It's not that we have different definitions of danger; in fact, they're quite similar, but we apply them differently in our lives. I know danger isn't the only agent of change, nor the best, but it delivers pleasure unfailingly.

Eric and I sat facing each other in kitchen chairs. We never usually did that—it's just how we ended up sitting. There was nowhere else to look except at each other.

Do you really need to know what happened to you?

Yes. I need to know if I was abused or not. And if so, then how.

Why does it matter?

Because I feel like a survivor, and if I actually am one, I want to live the life of a survivor. I think that's a pretty normal feeling to have.

Okay. But have you considered this: What happens if it turns out to be true? Won't you become an angrier person?

What are you talking about? I wouldn't try to take it out on people. I would get over it and try to make something beautiful with it. I'm aware of the need to end the cycle of abuse.

You don't know how you'll feel. No one can predict that sort of thing. What if it was something really bad?

I promise not to have a nervous breakdown if it turns out to be really bad. Is that what you want to hear? And what do you mean by "angrier"? Do you find me angry to begin with? Am I an angry person?

That's not what I'm saying. Isn't this all about forgiveness?

Yes, of course.

And isn't it easier to forgive now that you don't know what it is?

Ah...I see where you're going, but, um, knowing is the entire point. The forgiveness has to, um, mean something.

And sorry to get in your face about this, but what about the definition of abuse? It's not universal. I'm trying to be sensitive here, but this is such tricky territory. It's *nuanced.*

Hey. Saying something is "nuanced" doesn't add the nuance you're looking for. You don't support me. I can feel it.

I support you, I really do. But I want to be sure you know what you're doing. Sometimes I'm not convinced you think the present is more important than the past. That all you've lived counts for much, much more than whatever you're trying to remember.

Then you don't fully support me.

What are you afraid of?

Losing my memory. Maybe that's why I'm doing this now,

before I forget too much. And I'm afraid of losing my stutter after all this time. I'm afraid of becoming fluent. These days, when I tell people I stutter, they say they didn't know until I said the word "stutter." They have no right.

Ha. You don't stutter like you used to, but you still have it, honey.

You're so encouraging.

What else?

That's not enough?

Here's what I think. I think you've been avoiding the topic of your mother. That's where the answers lie. It's so clear to me, but it's like you're making yourself blind to it on purpose. Of course it'll be painful, but that's part of the work.

I got up to make some tea, although Eric was usually the one who made it, so I didn't know where anything was. I just stood at the counter hovering in front of the cupboards, hoping the tea bags, cups, and saucers would materialize.

What's up with you today?

They changed stuttering to Childhood Onset Fluency Disorder in the DSM-5. The American Psychiatric Association still lists it as a mental fucking illness.

And you have a problem with that.

Yes, I have a fucking problem with that. I have a problem with, um, being another acronym. I'm already identified by so many acronyms, I don't think I...jeez! I *can't* take another. And stuttering never should've been on the disorder list in the first place.

I don't think there's anything wrong with you. But I can see the value of having it on the list. Like maybe it opens up funding. Or something?

Funding.

Yes.

Fuck funding. And fuck the DSM-5.

Everybody needs money, even to do the noblest things. The speech therapy industry needs government funding to function. Some people want to be helped. But it looks like you don't.

I accept help. I just don't want to be pathologized anymore.

Did—what was her name, the speech therapist—

Rosa.

Did she ever pathologize you?

Yes, but it wasn't her fault, it was just her job. That's what they all do. For the money.

Listen, you can move on with your life and pretend speech therapy hasn't helped you. That's your prerogative.

This is really surprising coming from the President of the Deaf and Dumb Society. It's as if you think signing your way through everything doesn't make you look like a moron.

Hey. That was mean.

I'm sorry, but if stuttering turns out to be a mental illness, I mean if it's actually, um, a self-protection mechanism, a childhood onset whatchamacallit, a symptom of abuse, a bruise, if you will, then I'm screwed. Because I'm *proud* of my stuttering. It's part of who I am. It's my identity. I've learned how to accept my speech as a bent part of myself. A queer part. It's a difference in me. My signal is jammed, and I wouldn't have it any other way. But I'm conflicted that I identify so strongly with, like I said, a mark of abuse. Unless I was destined to become a stutterer anyway? Which is a distinct possibility. I don't know anymore. I don't know anything.

You think you were born this way? Sounds like gay essentialism to me.

I don't care for your snotty analysis. This is really hard for me.

Well, don't take it out on me, asshole, or I might not stick around to help you through it. Find yourself a fucking therapist.

Then stop acting like one. If you really want to know what I'm afraid of, it's inventing memories that never existed. I've done it before. I could be making myself so impressionable that any idea could seem like a memory, and soon I'll be full of false ones. Next thing you know, I'll be saying Big Bird made me grind on his face. No, I'm not kidding. This is how people get falsely accused, and it happens all the fucking time. They go to jail for nothing. Now you know. And maybe now you can stop bugging me.

Are you talking about your imaginary friends again?

FUCK. YOU. GO FUCK YOUR FUCKING SELF.

I had long resisted seeing a psychotherapist or other type of counsellor to talk about things that were on my mind. Perhaps it's because I have a harder time confiding than most people. Who knows what biases a therapist has, sitting there judging you silently while you let your emotions crawl on the carpet in front of them like a sick, maimed animal? I've heard others say with relief that they feel free to tell strangers anything, knowing they'll never see them again. I retort that they'll most definitely see a stranger again, that when a comet passes you, it's not by accident. Once you're in someone's orbit, it's hard to avoid them. I wish they were right, that we'd see strangers only once and never again. If that were the case, I'd empty myself into them to the very bottom and then run away just before they exploded with an overload of human goo. I would use the situation to my advantage. But that's not how it works.

Memory. I don't understand it. It's not a video recorder with a tape you can just play back; it's more like the highs and lows of life get stamped into blood and tissue particles like icons imprinted onto tabs of ecstasy, which then float away into remote corners of the brain until a weak signal is sent to retrieve them. A memory can totally mutate on the way back or melt away completely. Maybe forgetting is a good thing. Our minds must do it for a reason. Maybe memory is a giant storage warehouse that bombs itself to hell every year to make room for new stuff. Who knows? How could I possibly trust a therapist to muck around in there? With my luck, I'd be bound to meet someone who earned their diploma with a save-the-children thesis on how every element of human behaviour can be explained by past trauma, so that when they find a trace of trauma, it never occurs to them they might have accidentally implanted it there.

For the record, it's official: Yes, I welcome danger to fuck up the elements of my life that have become too static to be useful. I welcome it to completely dismantle everything I love because I know the reward for something that painful must be exceptionally good. My most dangerous ideas are also my most creative, and restricting them to nighttime agonies and compartments of paranoia cannot possibly be useful to me. I wonder how truly creative I am, if I even have the visionary faculties to imagine my own disappearance, the death of old versions of me, as an extreme act of transformation, the unique chance to learn something about myself in a different world, far from the monotonous and stupid. All the meaningless fears that grip us at random moments but that don't actually matter are just the inner walls of a brain that hasn't learned to think big and beyond self-criticism and endless boredom. Bring me danger and bring it *now*.

Maybe I'm too dense to realize that Eric welcomes danger into relationships too, if this is what we've come to. Sometimes I have to remember that we're broken people, Eric and me. I have to forgive us for that. We're broken people looking for answers.

But after our argument, I was too angry to consider that. I decided to cool off by writing a letter to somebody else. A guy two boyfriends back.

Dear First Boyfriend,

It has been a long time. Your face is still fresh in my memory, every one of your smoking wrinkles, smiles meant for me or otherwise, but I forget your name. I remember it was rhythmically pleasing. It was at the bottom of every postcard you insisted on sending to me, even though we only lived a few doors away from each other.

I'm well (I think). How are you? To me, you're a ghost. You haunt me with the memory of my former self. I hope this Hotmail address still works. I am writing to apologize to you. You see, there's a chance that I'm damaged goods, as they say in the furniture moving business, and perhaps also in the industries of the heart.

In telling you this, I'm saying that what happened was probably not your fault. Absolve yourself, if you haven't already.

When I recoiled from you in bed, preferring the coldness of the wall to the warmth of your breath, that wasn't a conscious choice, but rather, it was informed by the museum of my past. When I refused to kiss you in public in a place where it made sense to do so, I didn't intend for you to go kissless, made a fool of. When I treated your affection as though it were a plastic bag coming to suffocate me, when I spun your shows of affection as tools of control and then allowed that to bloom into distrust, when I rebelled against you as if I were your child, that wasn't me—it was the things I was escaping. Am still escaping. Or trying to, at least.

You had no way of knowing that I was damaged goods. I apologize for not letting you see my struggle, for in hiding that, I became a mystery to you, and unlovable. When someone has a secret to hide, they usually cover up more than they mean to, to make sure the secret doesn't get out. I'm sorry for robbing you of someone knowable, for the theft of me from you.

Maybe you just thought I was an asshole.

That's only half the story.

What do I mean by damaged goods? I'm still working on that. Expect a second email. You are a precious and painful memory that I need to quell like a headache. Maybe you have become a hatred, and that is all we are to each other now.

I must get to the real apology, to the story of damage and all of its collateral representations. Think back:

To hide my own damage, I broke things around us,
pretended we were broken, that our union was pure
disrepair. Beyond fixing. I projected the museum of me
onto our relationship, and it crumbled in our hands.
You never knew the weight that was crushing us. I
never answered your questions—they were piercing
and heartful, but I pretended that they were misguided.
And here comes the most painful confession: It took you
only a few words to reach into the core of me, to the self I
couldn't deal with.

You came too close to the me that I couldn't face. And
so I broke us. I threw us out. That time we got "evicted,"
all of our stuff thrown crashing to the sidewalk—that
wasn't the landlord tossing us out because of unpaid rent.
Our clothes lay on the sidewalk, mashed into the mud in
the shape of boot treads, and our vinyl records tossed from
the landing were smashed under their own weight, a
constellation of shards. We were suddenly without music,
and every appliance was reduced to a mini hardware
store of its own components. You stared at me with the
hopelessness of having to rebuild our home from scratch,
so devastated that you actually still envisioned me in
your future. Newsflash: Our rent was paid on time,
and it wasn't the landlord, it was me who put us on the
street. I was so desperate not to be damaged goods that I
tried to damage everything else as an act of camouflage. I
hope you don't find it gauche of me, at this time, after all
this, to show you the poem I wrote for you that day. The

last poem I ever wrote. More of a song lyric. I'm already embarrassed by it, but here it is, because I'm certain you'll never speak to me again.

> *watching your fingers trawl through our stuff*
> *discovering newly the shape of things upside down*
> *as if you didn't belong in your own life*
> *made me hopeful that you could learn the lessons of*
> *pain*
> *I wondered if I had devised the perfect exit from you*
> *to go examine myself in the pain of peace*
> *but throwing objects you are never free of the*
> *memory of their weight*

> *Dear First Boyfriend: Were you really the first, my first? Do you want to be half of the first relationship I destroyed? After all this time, I don't know what your ego can support. And the truth: I can barely remember your face.*
> *I hope to God this is the right email address.*
> *I cannot imagine ever writing this again. No matter who it's for.*

When I was done, I saved the letter in my Drafts. I never sent it to my first boyfriend because as soon as I was done, I knew I had written it to Eric.

DANS LA FOSSE AUX LIONS

I had volunteered at CKUT for more than six months. The deejays had grown to like and even respect my programming. I'd find little smiley faces on Post-it notes where my blue sticker choices used to be. Were they the thieves? Corrupted by the thick blood of kin, I looked the other way.

Processing all this new music was having a dramatic effect on me. This reckoning with the self was too graphic, too much. Of course, I found every memory except the one I was trying to locate.

One day, we got the most curious package. An oversized Kraft envelope. I thought I recognized the handwriting: shaky, cursive, sloping, and hard to decipher. It suggested someone to me, although I couldn't figure out exactly who. My life seemed to be a litany of people who forever floated on this periphery of recognition.

It wasn't a package from a record label promoting new material, nor was it from the artist themselves. No sycophantic letter or other markings. Inside was a vinyl 45 of a Marilyn Monroe song. We never got old music like that.

I finally understood why I was alone in that cubicle: Sometimes you need to be in a small, enclosed space when big realizations come to you so you can grasp them before they dissipate into the atmosphere. Sometimes you must be in a pressure cooker with your own shock because it's good for you. My cubicle didn't have a turntable, so I went to an adjacent listening booth to find one. It had been awhile since I had handled vinyl. I'd forgotten how ritualistic the experience was: pulling the sleeve out of the jacket, then the record out of the sleeve, holding it at the edges to avoid smudging, laying it on the turntable just so, affixing the 45 RPM adapter to hold it in place, spinning the disc to remove dust with an anti-static brush, dropping the needle exactly where the song should start so there's no time spent waiting, missing it by a few seconds, and trying again.

Although well outside my preferred decade, it was an exquisite listen.

Marilyn Monroe. Yes, I used to be her.

It's funny trying to remember little boy experiences in the larger and much emptier mind of a man. It's hard to explain the blank pages in my story.

Who had sent the envelope? Nobody aside from Eric even knew that I volunteered at the station.

I needed a drink, so I walked down to the *Vieux-Port* to nose out a bar. I found one on rue Saint-Paul festooned with old empty wine bottles lining the walls, all the way up to the ceiling. I made my way to the back of the bar by instinct, to the sound of people talking in low voices, which dropped off completely when I came in. The small room was full. There was only one free table near the piano, so I took it. I ordered a beer and sat sipping it. People smoked.

A strange man approached me. At first I mistook him for a waiter, but then he sat at the piano right in front of me. The man was dressed in red velvet rags carefully sewn together into what resembled a tuxedo. It was trimmed with brocade and had a Nehru collar. Mother-of-pearl buttons ran halfway up the sleeves. The suit fit him impeccably but was covered in dust or maybe silica, what looked like sparkles, and cigarette ash. From where I sat, I could smell expensive French cologne and rotten milk. His hair was a greasy pompadour, arranged cavalierly and with a flourish. There was an immaculately pressed and starched white handkerchief tucked into the front pocket of his suit. This spectre held himself with the air of a king, a corpse, a Mozart aged like old cheddar. His face was carved with wrinkles and knife scars that were impossible to tell apart. His eyes I did not see.

The pianist started to play Jacques Brel as I drank my beer. After a few songs, he paused to smoke an unfiltered Gauloise *bleue*. I figured I could hazard a question.

Vous connaissez les chansons de Hall & Oates ?

Les Halles et Utz ? C'est qui, ça ?

Un groupe américain.

Pardon, mais je n'écoute pas la télévision… Croyez-moi, je ne connais pas ces conneries, quoi. Vous m'avez pris pour un con ? Allez vous faire voir avec ces trucs américains…

Sorry for asking.

Zut !

He turned his back to me dismissively to make love to his cigarette, and make love he did, fellating every puff of smoke like a gentle and experienced lover, with the doting concern of an old man. I could not immediately understand the difference between his roughness and his softness.

Vous connaissez les chansons de Marilyn ?

He turned to me, and I finally saw his watery eyes, melted in his head like raw oysters. They were ugly but kind. He nodded as he took a drag and blew smoke in my direction almost artisanally.

Mais oui, bien sûr et certain, mon beau… Pourquoi vous ne m'avez pas dit ça avant, hein, bijou ? Vous allez me faire pleurer… Alors, laquelle chanson ?

"My Heart Belongs to Daddy."

Merveille… vous me faites fondre.

The pianist started to play the song, and I have to say, I almost didn't recognize it without the horn section. It was lugubrious and slow and I think he played it that way deliberately. He wanted to throw me off. That's what I accused this pianist, this beautiful and hideous stranger, of trying to do. After my high school band had dissolved, I vowed never to sing again, but I could feel a change of wind in the waft of cigarette smoke. After all, I had something to prove.

I jumped up on the table, swaggering on the creaking oak. The patrons froze and stared up at me. Head pointed at the ceiling, I opened my throat and let it out. I began to unfurl the tongue from my mouth and sing a song to set our woes on a sailing ship. I sang hard. My heart belonged to daddy, but it also belonged to everyone in the bar.

At the next table, six men in their eighties were drinking pints of 1664. It was clear that they'd borne the sadness of war and that they'd been filtering it through decades of alcohol. They were waiting to see me entertain the troops one last time, or perhaps they were waiting for a young fellow Canadian to storm the beach.

Six men went erect.

Six beer glasses clinked.

Five men crawled around the table on goat legs and bleated.

One came around the back and stuck ten dollars down my pants.

Four men tried to sing along into a microphone of suds.

Lost two men to uncontrollable weeping.

Smiles all around.

Some liked it hot. All of them liked me.

Diamonds are a girl's best friend, I had to remind them.

Nobody did Montreal like Marilyn.

When I was done, I got down off the table and took my seat. There was applause and the pianist winked at me, but I was sad. I looked at the strangers around me, and I considered the tragedy of the people I had never met. Their stories were so similar to mine, but I would never hear them told. It would take a hundred lifetimes of random bar encounters to hear them all.

The pianist didn't have a tip jar, so I bought him a Pernod by way of thanks. He decided to play me out with "You've Got a Friend" by Carole King. He lurched into an aching instrumental version of it, all broken chord changes and heart strings. He played it wistfully and almost without rhythm.

I had to piss something wicked, but the bathroom was *hors ser-vice*. I went outside to the alley, unzipped, and started to let it out. Soon someone unzipped beside me. I stared at the penis and at the gnarled fingers holding it. The pianist was pissing in concert with me. Condensation rose like curls of cigarette smoke. His dick—had I seen it before? Hard to say.

Tu pisses comme si tu n'avais rien bu… Il faut lâcher contre le vent ou bien le garder dans ton pantalon. Do you live around here?

N-n-n-nnnon.

Ah, un petit chaton loin de sa mère. You stutter… *que c'est mignon*… too cute.

Unless I'm mistaken, I know you from somewhere.

Si, tu ne te trompes pas. But you are quite drunk, Marilyn, *n'oublie pas… Écoute, tu devrais passer chez moi pour un verre.* It seems like you have something… *comment peut-on dire,* to work out, *quoi?*

Why did I go home with him? It could be that I detected the delicate strains of BDSM in him. It's hard to know when I became curious about the taste for punishment, when I got the idea to teach myself lessons about physical pain and anguish and put myself through it all, knowing I would learn nothing and merely cover myself with meaningless bruises, the jagged edges of my scars unreadable, healing or not healing. Or perhaps it was inevitable that I gravitated to extremist views regarding sensation. I had soft-pedalled and dismissed them for years, and now was the time to call bullshit on that stance and throw myself into a final crucible, test the volume of my cries, the limits of my pain. I needed to inflict upon myself the cruellest elements of speech therapy. How far into darkness could my imagination go?

Luckily, the world is full of people skilled in the art of sexual exorcism. They can wrench a cry from deep in the soul, pull sweet music from unrefined pain just before the victim passes out, and bring them closer to ecstasy and god and death and the sun than they could ever go by themselves. Take it to the liminal.

Luckily, there are people who enjoy making this happen.

When we got to the pianist's apartment, a surprisingly boring and conventional-looking place, I told him I wasn't there for sex. He just smirked at me, said everything we do is for sex, and asked me if I wanted a glass of wine. I asked him what kind. He led me into his wine cellar, which through its coldness and vastness, its global selection of vintages and regions and grapes, and its refinement of storage practices, utterly silenced me. This seemed to please him.

He led me deeper into the cellar, into the mist of my own fear. I knew him from somewhere, this mystery just a few feet ahead of me, the long unwashed hair, the slouch that held sadness a certain way. The problem with strange men was that I seemed to recognize them all. I was a victim of my own desperation for answers. I followed, unable to resist his pull.

Perhaps I had been reading too much Gaston Leroux.

We had walked the distance of at least one Metro station, past millions of dollars of rare wines, and I didn't know where he was taking me. Without pause, he grabbed a bottle of 1982 Mouton Rothschild, broke the neck off by smashing it on the low stone ceiling, and offered me a swig. I told him I didn't drink cabernet but could make an exception. I downed half the bottle as we headed through an unlit corridor into a colder part of the cellar, deeper underground. I could feel the earth closing in over us.

I was unusually hard.

We finished another bottle of wine together. I shivered through the last dregs. The pianist had built a tunnel at least three Metro stops long, his own *catacombes*. I wondered what price I would pay for seeing something so secret. I soon got the feeling I couldn't afford it.

The tunnel ended, and we came to a high-ceilinged chamber cut into the stone of the earth. Calcite deposits decorated the walls. It was both primitive and majestic, like *le Stade*, in a way. I could tell by the chisel marks that he'd carved it out by hand. I turned to the pianist and suddenly felt a great compassion for him, for the loneliness it took to create a place of such darkness and beauty. He had even recreated parts of *Cimetière du Père Lachaise*, my favourite. Broken headstones poked out of the floor here and there, wrapped in the undergrowth of time, plants and flowers that bloomed without daylight and wrapped around the birth dates of the dead. The smell of decay.

The pianist led me to a stone slab, the kind popular at morgues in the world above. He laid my head on a granite pillow; it was the softest substance I had ever felt graze the baby hairs on the back of my neck, and it lulled me to sleep.

When I awoke, I found my host hovering over me, his oyster eyes dripping tears onto my folded hands. My first thought upon waking: Where was his piano? Didn't he own one?

Qu'est-ce que tu veux faire ce soir, mon beau ? Ne te gêne pas, petit garçonnet, j'ai tout entendu… Nothing can shock me at my age, *quoi*.

Do you know how to work a soldering iron?

Bien sûr, sois sans crainte—alors, pourquoi ? Non, non, laisse-moi deviner …

I explained to him how it was going to work: I would tell him a story. He would listen to the letters I stuttered on and brand them into my back with the soldering iron. Then he would force me to tell the story repeatedly until I got it right. We both knew the game could go on forever. We both knew that stutterers, no matter what kind of treatment they received, couldn't be reformed.

Perhaps I had been reading too much Franz Kafka.

The pianist prepared his accoutrements like he was setting a table for dinner. He laid out, with perfect etiquette, the soldering iron, an assortment of ointments and gels, and a white cloth napkin, and nothing was out of place. He had clearly done this many times before and was a trained minister of pain. With utmost delicacy, and humming a tune to himself, the pianist plugged the soldering iron into the rock, which was wet with sewer water. I would surely die of electrocution if not blood loss.

Tourne-toi, Marilyn ... Montre-moi ton dos.

I turned onto my stomach. He buckled me in with straps and covered me in ointment. He brought a bit of wine to my lips in the palm of his hand. I refused it. I wanted to focus on the proceedings and resign myself fully to them. For my story, I started to recite the Book of Daniel. The pianist started to brand me right away. I bucked against the leather straps. I recited and he seared me without cease. My mistake, going into this, is that I had expected breaks. But there was no reprieve or pardon. Even when I thought my speech was smooth, it turned out to be illusory because he didn't stop. No way out of this cellar except through my skin. I grimaced and babbled through beasts of the sea and the Son of Man, the feast of Belshazzar, the prophecies, the promises. Daniel had related these dreams to unbelievers, gifts of heaven that they paid back with ridicule. He died unfulfilled, promised heaven but rejected on earth. I tried to relate the story faithfully, but I failed miserably with a mouth unholy. The pianist carved letter after letter into me, starting a new one as soon as he finished the last. Hesitation was not in his repertoire. He engraved deeply. It felt like a forked tongue planting evil deep inside me, filling me with sex and lust and murder and greed and rebellion and disobedience.

Then my mouth told a story I'd never heard before.

Your Holiness,

Father, esteemed Judge and Jury, and Representative of the Almighty on Earth, it is not without extreme Trepidation that I come before You today, contrite and aware of your Schedule and Commitments as they pertain to overseeing the unrighteous Souls of the Flock, mine not excluded, and those, no less, of the World over; But if I, as Magistrate of the Court and your Servant, did not bring this perfidious and troubling Matter to your Attention, given its Severity and Implications, I would be lacking in my Duties;

His Holiness is no doubt aware of the Affliction of Stammering on certain wretched Souls, whereby the Tongue, born as a sacred Vessel in the Service of the Lord, embryonic and formless, shaping its first Utterances around Praise of the Almighty and all His fine Works, and whereby this original and unquestionable Function now ceases to operate as intended, but instead, has procured for its Owner a truly horrifying Spectre of Maladies, presenting in the Patient the following Symptoms;

*Blocks, Repetitions of the most inane Sort,
uncontrollable Drooling, Hesitations, and other lack
of Commitment, Squirming of the Lips, interminable
Prolongations, overall Laziness, Lack of Clarity,
uncontrollable Spittle, muscular Contortions, Rigor
Mortis of the Face, Paralysis of the Jowl, Wasting of
Time better spent in the Service of the Church, Inability
to express Piety as a natural Expression of facial Rest,
shut Eyes, and an Inclination toward Sodomy, Rape,
Incest, Lust, Murder, Gluttony, Insubordination,
Hubris, and especially Paedophilia;*

*Let the Record show that we believed the Patient
to be, according to our Assessments, curable, if not
completely, then at least mostly, for his Devotion to the
Father, Son, and Holy Spirit remained high, and we
initially perceived the diseased Patient as nothing more
than one of the Unfortunates, who perhaps contracted the
Illness through Parasites, which, by way of Explanation,
we know to originate in Water not blessed for the Clergy
for Use, or perhaps by the thoughtless and accidental
Overcooking of Meat, or some such other pedestrian
Stupidity to which the Masses are prone;*

*Therefore, we strapped the Patient into the dental
Chair, and with Tongs applied the traditional Leeches
to the Tongue, which siphoned out such a large Quantity
of obviously poisoned Blood through the diseased Organ
that the Patient passed out in Relief; Within a few days,
however, the Illness returned, so Garlic and Vinegar and*

Rounds of bovine Urine were poured into the Throat
of the Patient, who demonstrated Signs of Progress
including Vomitations that rendered his Body once again
pure and worthy of Service to the Lord; The Ailment,
however, persisted;

The pianist continued to melt holes in my back. My dick grew
so swollen under me that it hurt. Pre-cum flowed out and onto the
slab in a thin liquid sheet. I was leaking sweet pleasure.

It is around this Time that a Conclave of medical
Professionals was formed to analyze the Case; from afar
were called an equine Veterinarian of the highest Repute,
a Barber trained in the Art of Antiseptic, a Blacksmith,
and a Priest; there could be no Discussion with the
Patient, for obvious Reasons, so the Conclave, based on
observing excess Liquid under the Tongue, inability to
form clear Thoughts, Stamping of the Foot, Gyrations
of the Chin, and Resistance to previous Treatments,
amongst other abominable Symptoms, proceeded to
diagnose Mental Disorder;
It was clear at this Time, Your Holiness, that only
the calm Salvation of the Holy Scriptures could cure such
a Case, so we proceeded in Haste to the Church; We could
not take the Risk of leaving a Mental Disorder uncured
for too long, lest the Door to Contagion be left wide open
to ravage the Faithful like an unchecked Ague; It was
a Tuesday night at ten o'clock, so the Deacon had to be

*awoken from Slumber and this, to his Credit, he did
most graciously; The Patient was led into the Church to
the front-most Pew, where he was made to kneel and
recite to us from the Book of Psalms to calm the Torment
of his Soul;*

My testicles roiled in their pouch, and my groin fizzled with electricity. The pianist had figured out the contact points in my circuitry and was playing me like a theremin. I cried between sentences: Cum! Cum! Cum! Drown me inside out!

*It is at this Moment when the most disgusting
Display occurred, vile and unspeakable and in the most
sacred of Places, no less, verbal Eruptions of a decidedly
demonic Nature, for rather than read the placid Tidings
of the Book of Psalms, the Wisdom of Job to give Respite
and Balance to his diseased Mind, this Creature, no
longer human but as debased as an Animal, began to
speak in Tongues, babbling Nonsense that could have
no other Source than Satan the Devil himself; This was
confirmed when he began to recite, with perfect Fluency,
I swear upon these selfsame Holy Scriptures, the Book
of Revelation, the unspeakable Visions, Terrors, Spells,
Potions, Warnings, Prophecies, Incantations, Hexes,
and Demonisms, which, once spoken aloud, gives one
the Mark of the Beast and presents irrefutable medical
Evidence of Possession; We commenced posthaste in the
Cellar with the following Treatments, in Sequence:*

Flogging, Electrocution by Eels in a salt Bath,
Laxatives, Piercing of the Tongue with hot Needles,
Removal of the Epiglottis, Freezing of the Extremities,
Placement of a glowing Coal into the Mouth and
sealing it shut with a leather Bandage, and finally,
when nothing Else failed to release the Demon, when it
continued trying to speak through its earthly Mouthpiece,
complete Excision of the Tongue;
    Your Holiness, I report to You that the Patient did
not survive the Procedures, but it should come as no
Loss to the Church, as the Patient revealed himself to be
nothing more than a Tool of Beelzebub.

I opened my eyes and saw that for the entire last part of my incantation the pianist had moved away to do some housekeeping. What the fuck?

The very idea that I had stopped stuttering, if it were indeed true, made me feel like a beast losing its footing on a cliff and falling, falling, falling, then exploding into demon guts at the bottom of a gulch.

I couldn't take it.

I came and came and came and came and came and came until I was a puddle of semen and blood.

My back was a lacerated mess; it felt simultaneously like razor burn, frostbite, pins and needles, and the residue of a vicious spanking. The pianist unplugged the soldering iron. I felt his smile fill the room. He disinfected my wounds with lemon juice and salt. I cursed him out for a solid five minutes. He eventually unstrapped me.

Ma chérie, quelle coincidence that the two letters that give you ze most trouble are my initials. *C'est rigolo, quoi...*

What are your initials, you fucking demented motherfucker?

Zut!

What did you write on my back?

He never told me. The pianist simply bandaged me up in silence and saw me out. I had to fumble my own way to daylight, swathed in gauze, dizzy with pain. I would never forget him, but I couldn't come back. Then I felt bad, I felt sorry for this creature of the *souter-rain*, because it was his loneliness that drove him to these cruelties, his sadness that could fill endless quantities of underground caverns. This phantom knew everything about me, but I knew nothing about him.

When I got home, I removed the bandages and looked at the words in the mirror, which, of course, were backwards:

GNOS NWO RUOY KCIP

REFERENDUM QUESTION

Do you agree that, after having offered a formal economic and political partnership to Non-Stutterers, which includes but is not limited to: the understanding that eye contact shall remain unbroken for a minimum of thirty seconds until the stuttered sentence is out, that classroom policy will be reformed so that students are no longer failed when they refuse to speak in front of the class, the immediate elimination of any assumption of fluency superiority, whether physical, mental, or developmental, the banning of knowing glances traded between Non-Stutterers when a Stutterer among them is speaking, the abolishment of the automatic assumption of guilt among parents, a mutual acceptance of guilt for verbal misunderstandings, the prioritization of writing over speech, the creation of pitiless zones, self-determination of the stutterer, recognition of non-verbal stuttering in a variety of physical manifestations, the understanding that stuttering may occur in one language and not necessarily preclude fluency in another, that the reason for a stutter may change over the years, that there may never be a knowable reason, and that is acceptable, that Stutterers shall declare sovereignty?

   ◯ OUI

   ◯ NON

REQUIEM

I spent a week making sure he would be hungry. This meant a calculated control over the contents of the fridge and the cupboard. I
made sure that at least one key ingredient was missing from each
of his favourite meals. We had white wine, pasta, and primavera
sauce kicking around, so I made sure to dump the shrimp tails in
a discreet vortex flush and then disinfect the toilet bowl rim for
smell, scales, and other evidence. I found ground beef, hamburger
buns, and pickles so I gave the bread crumbs to the birds. Faced
with cereal and milk, I buried all of our spoons in the bottom of the
neighbour's trash can.

These means weren't excessive, considering that Eric was a
master at spoiling his dinner a few minutes before it was served.
Besides, on that particular night, I needed his full attention. Gaining
control of his stomach was the quickest way to assure that.

When lobsters hiss in a pot of boiling water, that's not air escaping out of their shells. We all know they scream.

And perhaps they screamed even more loudly when, on their

trip from the bathtub to the kitchen, they caught glimpses of a room decorated with floral arrangements, including the most grotesquely large hibiscus in free-range bloom, dripping deep red like aging blood and hung from track lighting, or when they saw the chef ignoring them to prepare a saltwater reflecting pool in the corner composed of igneous boulders hewn from Mount Royal after scrubbing off the squeegee-punk graffiti, or when, at last, the chef laid them in a bath of St. Lawrence River water, placed just so in a plastic pool from Canadian Tire, to which he added Greek sea salt from Arahova Souvlaki on rue Saint-Viateur. Or perhaps they were screaming in protest upon seeing the lobsters I had placed in the reflecting pool that would remain alive. I didn't put them there to mock our dinner catch, I swear.

Anyway, I'd like to think that this all hurt me more than them. My back lacerations were still healing. Every twist opened me right up.

While dinner made dinner noises, I adjusted the bow tie on my tuxedo, finger-licked my eyebrows into submission, and arranged the table in the middle of the living room. I had procured a set of discontinued bone china from a housewares store in a decaying strip mall on the Decarie Expressway where they could get away with out-of-season stock. The beauty of these obsolete finds was that nobody else with taste had them, and I could be assured of a thoroughly fresh and original night with my baby. I installed a mirror ball on the ceiling to refract the brilliance of every moment and to light up the dozens of scraps of paper inscribed with Jean Genet quotes—from the sanguine to the vapid—that I had taped to the walls. I figured if I was to present my freedom to Eric over dinner, then we should at least be surrounded by representations of prison. If constraints press hard enough on a person, does liberation emerge, as coal under pressure produces a diamond? I can only imagine and hope.

I piled the table high with claws, mopping up the butter as it slathered off the table and onto the floor, then skated on my socks over to the sound system, which I had slid into the centre of the living room just in front of the table. Our speakers weren't adequate so I'd rented a stack of Bose subwoofers and tweeters and arranged them concert-style around the table. I was going for volume, for whatever would blow my baby's mind and the whiskers off the crustaceans. In the war of self-discovery, there's no music etiquette I can abide by, and the neighbours could go to hell, if hell was a place worse than the dinner I'd designed.

I had lingering doubts about the success of the night. Eric could've stopped into any number of fast food places on the way home or eaten lunch too late or suddenly become vegetarian or simply come home too tired for dinner. The stakes were high: it would take something remarkable to keep him sitting still so he could feel the music that I wanted him to feel. It would take a multi-course meal of things he'd never tasted or seen before. It would take lobsters marinated in juniper and crème de menthe, with their shells dyed in Easter egg colours.

Fortuitous timing, it was. Just as Eric walked in the door, I laid the vinyl on the turntable, licked the needle for good luck, and dropped it a little too hard. The music stuttered from the first few seconds. Eric took off his shoes. He looked at The Little Mermaid swimming pool, perplexed, and yelped when an ambitious lobster that had escaped from the bathroom pinched his ankle and awaited retaliation.

Don't mind him. Things are a little crazy here. But you should sit down because dinner is starting to get cold.

It's not getting cold, it's attacking me. It smells garlicky in here.

All the better to kiss you with.

What's with the speakers? More deaf humour? If it really gets you off, I can remove my ears completely.

No need, but thanks.

I played side two of the Hall & Oates album *Bigger Than Both of Us* as a kind of prelude. I seated my guest, pushed in his chair, and gave him a dinner jacket so that my tuxedo wouldn't make him feel entirely out of place in his own home. We cracked shells together and pulled out the meat with lobster picks. I had also prepared a plate of long-grained rice and a wakame salad with sesame oil. There was a side of crackers.

In case you don't remember or have forgotten, like I did, the cover of the record shows Daryl and John sitting on a sectional sofa. John plays guitar while Daryl writes something in a book, perhaps lyrics or sheet music. Behind them, a mixing board landscape is visible through a huge bay window. There are avenues of faders with volume knobs at every intersection and apartments made of tuning needles stacked on top of each other. In front of them is a table with an open wine bottle and single wine glass, evidence that they shared such things intimately. The pièce de resistance is a box of Ritz crackers, a most curious and salty form of product placement, and definitely one of the more absorbing mysteries of the short but ostentatiously bright Rock and Soul movement.

There's a detail that's easy to miss if you don't look carefully: a pair of feet in high heels are crossed in the foreground, the presumption of an unseen woman just outside the frame.

Isn't there always an unseen woman?

I was getting turned on by how the butter collected in Eric's unshaven facial hair, by how much of dinner he missed through distraction, just by focussing his body on the bass in the speakers, listening to the music through the floor, how he subconsciously inched his chair ever closer. I adjusted the table with my toe to compensate. Soon we were right up against the music, and we started to fill our gullets with shelled lobster. (The crème de menthe was disgusting, even from a sexual point of view.) Eric was rocking to the music. The mirror ball dappled us with light.

I got up to flip the record.

Eric looked at me, wiping the cracker crumbs off his lips. He leaned over for a kiss. I could tell that he knew. He saw in my face that after all the work I had put into finding a phantom song, I had found nothing, and now I was just playing what I wanted.

I loved how his deafness made him study the emotion in my face. It was enough to make me fall in love with him every time.

TES ENFANTS LES TI-PAUVRES

Prayer to the Grand Antonio:

When you left us, you taught us how to be free. And long before that, too, *mon doux.*

Do you know that when I look into the eyes of a large animal or one that thinks it's bigger than small, one brave enough to live outside in the winter and lick its nose clean at the risk of freezing, one who picks a fight in the most desperate situations and wins...I look into its eyes and I see you?

It was hard to never hear you speak about World War II. What happened to you? Did you see everyone you love die? Were you unable to rescue them? Did it take the strongest person in the world to save them, and you weren't yet that strong? Did it confuse you, cause you anguish, that you couldn't repel the tanks with your shoulders? That you couldn't jam the shells back into the cannons with your fists? That your arms weren't big enough to stop your entire family from falling into a crypt, weren't long enough to pull them out?

That you spent the rest of your life pulling buses with your hair to make yourself as strong as your family had needed you to be?

We all had a theory. But we were all wrong. Because you never spoke about it, there was no past. The silence was as heavy as you were, and it crushed us. So, in our pain, we wrote prayers and mailed them to your office at the Dunkin' Donuts on the corner of Beaubien and Saint-Denis, hoping that one day you would answer us:

Dieu le roi
Antonio Barichievich
Dit Antonio de Montréal
Champion des champions
Embrasse-nous
Tes enfants les ti-pauvres
Tes enfants qui se souviennent trop
Champion du monde
Número un
Antonio de Montréal
Tes enfants qui sont esclaves du passé
Du passé présent, passé décomposé
Explique-nous la guerre, ce dégât
Soulage-nous, Dieu le roi

When you didn't answer us, we became kinder to animals. We started eating cloves of garlic by the wheelbarrow and ran head-first into tree trunks from sixty metres away. We blocked out the pain of your silence by growing our hair long and braiding it with black electrical tape. We became kinder to the animals of ourselves and learned to live outside.

And we began to forget our pasts.

For many of us, it started while watching the TV interviews you gave. Your answers changed. You said you were Siberian until you were transfused with Italian blood. Then you said you were Yugoslavian once Yugoslavia ceased to exist. There were whispers that you were Croatian. Suspicions that you were Slovenian. Rumours that you were Greek.

You set us free with every incoherent word that the microphone couldn't pick up. We burned our birth certificates in a garbage can at the corner of Beaubien and Saint-Denis and gave each other new names while we watched the heat melt the ice on the sidewalk.

We began to speak with echoes of strange new accents, inflections not our own. We turned questions down and statements up. With no prior addresses, we couldn't get jobs or new homes, and that's when we really started to take care of each other. We learned that there was always enough food to share, even for the hungriest alley cats.

Sometimes our mail came back from Dunkin' Donuts marked *"déménagé,"* so we took to taping our messages on the window, text facing in, hoping they'd stick and stay up long enough for you to see them.

We started to forget our own pasts, but we couldn't forget yours. Did you bargain with marauding soldiers to spare the lives of everyone in your village, promise a feat of strength only to miss it by a few kilos? Did you watch everyone get shot while you worked through a Charley horse? Could you not pull everyone to safety with your hair? Did the army reject you for some unseen infirmity? Were you not yet your own army?

Some of us changed when you claimed to be prehistoric, when

a woolly mammoth came alive in front of us, all yellowed tusks, ageless. You were an animal of shifting breed.

We couldn't bear the silence so we told each other constantly changing stories about our own pasts. Our backgrounds became fiction, but we learned to live them. In bars we reached into our pockets and produced watches, gold pendants, torn and faded photos, heirlooms that nobody gave us, stolen, borrowed, found, freed from hock. These random objects became who we were. We traded them for drinks and stories. We lent out our tree trunks indiscriminately.

Our stutters were born in countries without governments or flags.

We prayed to saints with names we couldn't pronounce.

We started to feel free from some of the pain. We started to write, and we learned with sadness that in some languages we didn't stutter, that we could stumble too quickly through the words, mouthfuls of liquid with nothing to chew on. We learned the curse of fluency.

We wrote prayers that were poetry, but junk mail to donut shop managers. When they tore our notes from the window, we began to gather in front of Dunkin' Donuts, paper shaking in hand. We read loudly in case you were nearby and could hear us:

Dieu le roi
Saint-Antonio des rêves
Dites-nous la vérité
Que le passé décomposé nous libère
S'efface-t-il lui-même ?
Oui, en toute beauté

Écrase-nous tes enfants
Écrase-nous quand tu dors
Notre mort nous libère
C'est du passé tout cela
Champion mondial, le plus fort des futurs
Explique-nous la guerre des mots
Antonio de Dunkin
Menteur número un
Tes enfants te croient de plus en plus
De moins en moins

Some of us changed when the price of donuts went up, when they kicked you out and explained it was a business decision, when you spent the following years sitting on the fibreglass bench outside as if you had always done that, as if a quickly cooling coffee had always been enough to keep you warm, as if you had not suddenly been put outside like an unwanted animal.

Some of us changed when you claimed to no longer be prehistoric but extra-terrestrial. Some of us had been waiting our entire lives for interplanetary contact. Others didn't know that our pasts could leave the earth. Of course you were an alien. What else could you have been?

All of us changed when we realized how easy it was to rewrite stories that no longer explained us. We finally understood that the war no longer explained you. A bomb cannot explode in outer space because there isn't enough oxygen. But donut sprinkles can float for light years.

I often think of your hands, how you laid them on my head all those years ago. As if you knew I would need the strength of a holy anointing. I've felt the promise of outer space ever since.

And I'm sorry for what I did. I should've defended you in the face of false accusations. I was distracted by root beer. But it's still no'excuse.

When you left, it was just another rewriting of your past. You were just leaving another war.

We would never hear from you again, no matter how many letters we wrote. But we would still write them.

And that's how we finally became free. Now we could leave home and not worry about losing it. Because there was nothing left of our home.

Mon Antonio, *mon doux.*

Where have you gone? We still can't take it.

FREEDOM OF INFORMATION REQUEST
1475997

"—the shortage of supplies. The weather changed rapidly, and we monitored it on the hour, made gains when we could, pushing forward a few hours at a time until night when we set up camp and tried to keep warm. Without much oil left, we had to burn shoe wax to thaw our fingers and toes and to cook. Frostbite set in, and some of our bravest lost extremities. To their credit, they did not complain despite the terrible disfigurement and, to avoid lowering the morale of our battalion, they did not cry during amputation. I hope their souls will be rewarded in heaven. There was more snow than expected. Our guns froze. The mechanisms did not fire, and we had no way to remove the frost that lined the cannon walls. At first we tried to do this with branches, but either the wood got stuck and caused further complications, or we ran out of trees. The war has destroyed the forest. A few soldiers died of hypothermia, and we had to leave them behind. We buried them in the snow, and a soldier whose uncle used to be a priest read them the Sacraments.

The worst was when they died while we were stuck at base camp, tank treads encrusted with ice and glued to the ground like houses. We had to sleep among the dead, and they invaded our dreams. In the morning, rigor mortis lifted their arms or legs into the air, poking through the shallow snow graves we had dug. One of the deceased gave us the finger. It was a sign. We tried to bury the dead face down, but then their posteriors poked through. We started to give confession to them just before they died. We told them our secrets so our secrets would die nose-down in the frozen ground and we would not have to carry them anymore. Anything to lighten the load. Many of us confessed to murdering when it was not necessary. Bayonets clean through children. Vengeance. Loss of control. In civilization, we kind of went crazy. In isolation, we went even crazier. You can say that it is the snow that has defeated our country. Foregone conclusion. We were indeed starting to lose morale. There was a shortage of food. We had a soldier who was proud of having never cried, but he blubbered like a baby the night he watched a friend spread dandruff on a piece of sponge like butter on toast. That little thing completely broke him down. Our batteries died and we lost radio contact. We should all have died at the time. The mortars exploded around us so often that we didn't notice the sound anymore. Or we had gone deaf. Without rescue or instructions, we considered retreat. After all, the war could've been over and we never would've known. But most of us were also snow blind and unable to identify forward or backward. Our maps were frozen, brittle, disintegrating. Our tools gave up on us. If we could move in any direction, either toward the enemy or away from them, then we had some hope of salvation, in either escape or capture. But we were immobilized in ice. The warmer days messed with our minds, the snow melting, then later, the water refreezing to ice before we had a chance to move on. Brief glimmers dashed instantly. Then there was the morning when everything changed. One of our own, fat and useless for most of the war, woke up early. I say this with all affection because we living remnants had grown quite comfortable speaking about each other this way. Not only fat and useless, he was also silent and lazy; we thought he'd been sent to war for being mentally ill, or maybe so he could mooch food and board. He used to speak to the dying as their blood froze, but we never heard what he said. We assumed he had more secrets than most, having a much bigger body. When he wasn't alone, which was most of the time, he shared his warmth. We used to gather around, three men under each arm. He allowed us the courtesy of pretending to sleep. So we learned to respect him despite his strangeness and despite the fact that he stank. We had completely run out of tank fuel. Almost no food left. Stuck until spring, which would be far too late for most of us. So we slept in our tanks and waited to die. We left the doors open so we could stare at a roof of stars, so we could count ourselves into permanent sleep. Sometimes we counted the stars, other times we counted the people back home. We said their names again and again, slightly changing them every time, until they were different people altogether and we could forget them in our hearts. It was rare that we all woke up alive, but one night, it happened. I no longer believed in God or humanity or peace or love, but I did believe in fortunate turns of good weather and all they make possible. We woke up to one such day. The sun was yellow and hot. Spring was a sudden blaze, an attack, which cleared the frost right out of our ears; we snapped just to make sure the sound was real. It was not the sound of the enemy coming to capture us. It was the sound of metal. We kept snapping to rule out the sound of shrapnel ricocheting through memory, but no, it was our man linking up the tanks with chains, like a row of army toys, and pulling them through the melting snow and the mud, the chain wrapped around his enormous hair and beard. He pulled us forward while sinking into the earth, burying himself alive so we might all be saved. And in no less than twenty-two languages he declared himself a war hero. Stupidly, we just kept snapping our fingers until he—"

THAW

BIGGER THAN BOTH OF US

Eric was right about my mom. He knew I needed to chisel her out of the ice in my head and ask myself the right questions. But it had to come back naturally. Well, one day, it did.

The image itself is fairly uncertain. I'm small and standing in front of a record player. The receiver is silver and covered with dials. There are tiny tuning meters in little glass windows filled with yellow light, stacked like apartments in a building. The needles wobble back and forth, showing the science of the music. In this image, I'm not sure what the song is. I'm staring at the record spinning on the turntable. The label hypnotizes me, creating a swirl of colour in my head that didn't exist before. The grooves orbit past me like black oil, smooth and perfect. I'm just discovering my relationship to the substance of vinyl. This record doesn't have any scratches. The arm bobs as the record turns. There's a slight warp. I want to see the needle up close so I pretend I'm tiny and jump onto the turntable in my mind. You might say I haven't come back since.

As soon as I land beside the arm and admire the boy-sized

diamond tip at my feet, I begin to feel I'm not alone. There's a presence behind me. Don't ask me what the clues are: shadow, body heat, breath on the back of my downy neck. For whatever reason, I don't want to turn around. Maybe it's because I know the music will stop.

There is indeed someone in the room with me.

It's odd to have a childhood memory in which there is no strange man present, but it comes to me as clear as ice. As clear as the ice that has melted and fallen off us. I see her long, flowing brown mane, the colours refracting in the sunlight like a prism over my shirt, tones of mahogany, apple, and wine, auburn radiant and captivating, parts of it golden like beer in a TV commercial, the memory of hair among the strongest I have, no mistaking it; the whole living room smells like her shampoo—she is no stand-in or imposter. She hears me calling her and comes close. A hug evaporates the dream and the fear, and I nestle into the crook of her neck, a soft blanket of curls, nuzzle deep inside the hidden wet strands, catch a taste of residual shampoo (wheat germ and jojoba, essential nutrients for a growing boy), and I can feel she has begun to hum the song that's playing for us.

What I've come to learn is that people are songs.

I pull away because I'm starting to suffocate, and I tell her all about the impossible and crazy things that happened. She's confused because we've been together all along, but there were things that happened in another world, in a world outside the living room and away from the music, away from the record player. I tell her about the ice dream, about the shivering coldness of it, and how I still can't get warm. I tell her about her her her her her her her her

her her her her her her. I tell her about the long search for a way out, the tributaries that I followed through the melting ice, traces of song, the inevitable refreezing and dead ends, how a scent can't go cold when it's already frozen. I tell her about getting lost in the streets of Montreal with boots on my hands to keep them warm, and it seems like she doesn't believe me.

I need her to believe me.

So I bring out the scientific evidence. I make her stop the music so I can tell her about my discovery. I fetch a postcard and bring it to her. It's a ratty piece of waterlogged cardboard with a photo of the specimen on the front. I explain how I discovered a woolly mammoth in the ice. I had been looking for her by scoping out traces of her hair, and instead I found this. It was a mistake, and it totally threw me off, just poking out, human-like, and with some of her colouring. In my desperation to connect, I reached out and grabbed it. I discovered a creature of a whole other sort, and once I had done that, I had to bring the scientific experiment to completion, to see what extinct animal I had awoken into the world.

I need her to believe me, so I grab her hand and drag her into the building hallway and down the stairs without our jackets. She thinks I'm crazy, but lets me lead her to the street corner where we chill by the fire hydrant, which gives me a sudden urge to take a leak. I tell her that he was just here, he's always here, and if we wait awhile, he'll come by. Right here on this bench. The bench is covered with snow and ice that hasn't been cleared since the season changed. We wait for about five or six buses to pass, squinting down the street for the tell-tale lights as each one approaches. We scan the windows for anything that matches the physical description

I've given, but each bus leaves us empty-handed. My heart becomes a glacier, and we walk back to the apartment.

I blow my nose and ask her, for the last time, if she believes me.

As her answer, she puts on a record by Buffy Sainte-Marie and smiles.

I smile back.

Then something happens. Our landlord is in the stairwell, and he's screaming about Swedish people coming here to steal our jobs. She knows what this means because she throws us into winter clothes and drags us onto an eastbound bus. We always find out about things at the last minute. But there's no snowfall heavy enough to make the distance from the West Island to downtown uncrossable. The bus gets stuck in the snow, so we jump up and down to keep warm, and we make snow angels to kill time. Then a replacement bus comes, which is driven by more of a singer than a driver, and he goes through half the ABBA catalogue because we're on the way to their concert at the Forum, and when we get there he parks half on the sidewalk and half on the street and tells us to save him a seat. Sure thing, buddy, we say. Sure thing. Then we hightail it through the front doors, and she tells the ticket taker that she's a friend of Benny Andersson and that he'd better let us in because nobody wants a sad Benny Andersson. That could be the ruination of ABBA, the end of our happy winters, she warns. He moves away, maybe because he can tell we'd hop over him like a turnstile if he didn't.

I ride her shoulders all the way up to the nosebleeds, where the drunks are swaying in the aisles with plastic cups of beer. We steal their seats but then decide to hang out with them on the cement staircase and scream out song titles, sure that our throaty requests from the 400 section will be heard and honoured, that our trip through the blizzard has given us the courage of volume, that it liquefies and spills out of us on its own frequency. It turns out we're right.

ABBA plays our song.

She looks at me, and at first I wonder if she's trying to tell me something. Maybe Benny Andersson has more secrets than we do. But then I realize the whole band is looking in our direction. They're looking right at us and so is everyone else, even the drunks, and then the spotlights hit, and we still have snow on our heads so we light up like disco balls and splinter the light back into the crowd. I can't believe this moment was here waiting for us, not only all night but also for the duration of my four-years-long life. We dance and people copy us.

Sadly, after you become an ABBA disco ball, the only way to go is down. Life will become a permanent fall from accidental pop stardom.

The snow eventually melts.

I'm not inclined to say what our song is. Mainly because I've already said too much.

CHIQUITITA

Of course she believed me.

Now that I think back, she knew about the existence of woolly mammoths and other incarnations that strange men took for camouflage or other reasons. Perhaps she was even hyper-aware of them.

For the first few years of my life, I observed her constantly looking at men. I just assumed she was man-hungry. But eventually, I figured out that she was watching out for me by watching out for them. When we were on the bus, and I busily validated paper transfers by feeding them into my mouth, she monitored the men around us, hiding under beards and clean-cut masks, behind sunglasses, reading past the pages of their books, signalling each other with their eyes. Their subtle body language. Men offered me candy all the time, and she slapped it to the floor as if they were handing me mustard gas pellets.

When I went to daycare so she could work, she skipped work to peer through the windows and make sure male janitors didn't sweep by me with their broom alibis. I imagine this surveillance got expensive for us. When the young man working at the ice cream parlour offered me an extra scoop for free, she whipped a Polaroid camera out of her purse and snapped his mugshot, no doubt for her album of budding pervs who wanted to get me. Doctors had to be women, and when they were men, she forbade them from checking anything unless I consented four or five times in complete, affirmative sentences that incorporated language directly from the question.

I have a feeling that most of her security work was done unseen. I imagine it was tireless and thankless and exhausting, and I'm sure I was a rotten little client.

I was a rotten little client who felt safe.

But I wondered why the security detail had to be so intense. Indeed, I did start to think I must have had diamonds or gold bricks in my gut, that possession of me was valuable in some kind of monetary way. Maybe I was money. Ever the patient one, she would sit me down and pull the scratched and creased Polaroids out of her purse and ask me if I remembered any of the faces. Yes, of course, these were the men she constantly yanked me away from, seconds before she snapped their sudden, perplexed frowns. Guilty by flashbulb. Then she compared them side-by-side to grainy black-and-white portraits in newspaper clippings, taken from the crime pages, which were always strangely adjacent to the comics. There were some similarities, but their ages confused me. Weren't these men little boys once, roughly my shape and size? She said, of course they were, but they'd been taken from their mothers.

Whenever we passed a woman on the street who was alone, she said, Aha! there's one whose boy was taken away. Where did the boys go? I started to peer into alleys and basement apartments, and I'd run into forbidden zones like men's rooms where I peered under every stall, curious to see where these lost boys of the city were. I began to suspect the boy mannequins at Eaton's and Simpsons of being boy-shaped cases where they were kept. I swore I could see them move sometimes.

I could slip through cracks quite easily.

I began to suspect that they kept lost boys at the zoo. There were plenty of places to hide them. Kids and animals weren't much different; we were monsters of similar size and temperament and went into cages when ordered to do so or were sometimes trapped in dens with each other. We visited *le Zoo de Granby* once, where she paid her own admission but told me to sneak behind her through the turnstiles.

Here's where the story gets weird, where it re-quantifies everything I know about music. I'm always weird about music; I'm sure it's a degenerative condition of some sort.

I remember her trying to teach me animal names. It didn't go very well because I called every animal I saw a chiquitita. Aardvark was a chiquitita. Emu was a chiquitita. Hippo was an exception because it was either a poppomis or a chiquitita. Everyone was a chiquitita, and it frustrated her.

As we passed the cages and pens and pits of chiquititas, I examined the enclosures for ways we could break in to kidnap them. But I just couldn't see it happening. The glass was too thick, the walls too high, the moats too deep. But then we saw butterflies in a greenhouse, and they looked catchable. She must've read my mind because she sat us on a bench and left her purse hanging wide open, an improvised lure. The understanding was that we were hunting or, more specifically, trapping. This was a secret, and we had to stay still; if we twitched even a muscle, everything would be over and people would know, and the poppomisses would eat us and maybe even worse.

After a long time, an exotic blue butterfly landed on the metal clasp of her open purse. Last of the species, I hoped. With a deft move she flicked it in with a fingernail and snapped the clasp shut.

With my cheek pressed against the leather, I serenaded the imprisoned butterfly, and the rest of my life began to fall into place.

I hoped that Chiquitita would tell me what was wrong

I was sad to see something enchained by its own sorrow.

As a little starlet, I started to demand that she be my personal paparazzo and constantly take my photo. Our relationship was changing; I became her client. I became a poseur, sidling up for photo ops with every dog we came across, comparing our panting tongues. I found celebrities on the street, and we posed for the most outrageous Polaroids. These were career-making shots that we later sold for a whole five bucks. We did Barbra Streisand, Leo Sayer, Patti Smith, and even some Québécois stars like Robert Charlebois and Ginette Reno before deciding it wasn't the career for us. A shame, because we were damn good at it. We eventually had to turn the celebs down. Peter Gabriel didn't take it well.

I wanted the simple life. My favourite thing in the world was to eat at the *casse-croûte* on l'avenue Papineau. It had posters of the Montreal Canadiens, a signed and yellowed photo of Yvan Cournoyer and Guy Lafleur eating smoked meat, shelves lined with giant jars of red bell peppers, and, near the window, a poster of

Andre Dawson that was so sun-exposed that all the reds had faded and the Expos uniform was white and blue. He could've been a Blue Jay. The smoking customers divided themselves into tribes: the Rothmans King Size, the Matinée Lights, Player's, Export A's, the Du Mauriers, the unfiltereds, a kind of royal family who all avoided each other expertly, a caste system delineated by booths. Because of these divisions, the ceiling panels above them were stained differently. You shall know them by their tar. They were sworn bowling enemies.

The Craven A's hated the Export A's for obvious reasons.

The booths had red vinyl benches and jukeboxes into which I plugged quarter after quarter to the electric hum of my little heart. I listened to the metal clink down through the machinery, then we chose our three songs with the numbered and lettered buttons. I didn't have to flip through the Rolodex of artists encased in glass. Not anymore. We knew what we wanted.

My favourite song was brought to us by the letter C.

Here, most of the rules regarding my safety didn't apply. It was a relief. The smokers winked at me and took turns having me in their booths, and that was okay with her. They were good people. I pillaged their poutines and stole their quarters, then came back to our booth covered in *sauce brune* and with a fistful of new music money. I was wrapped in the smoke of lovely older folks. These were my grandmothers and grandfathers, themselves wrapped in emphysema and Vicks VapoRub, and time slipped away. Coughing, choking, with crow's feet full of kindness and despair. I crept from tribe to tribe indiscriminately, yet they all trusted me implicitly. Nobody took me for a spy.

That night, we mucked around with Rush and Jim Croce for awhile, then Crosby, Stills, Nash & Young, John Denver, and Cat Stevens. I ploughed through a plate of greasy fries until my face was bloodied with ketchup. Then I saw a look come over her face. She stared into her purse. I assumed it had to do with the butterfly we had stolen earlier, and she said yes, it was dead, but that wasn't the point. The point was that it had munched through our paper money, leaving only the Queen's cheeks, her crown, and a few other bits and bobs. There was no money left to pay for the fries. We had spent the coins on music. I suggested we just leave, but she said that wasn't an option. These people knew us. We were in a situation.

I told her to get the camera ready.

"Chiquitita" started to play on the jukebox.

I stood on the table, and the other diners all turned to look. I opened my heart to the music, displayed all of my songbird feathers. My tears weren't crocodile, they were real. I was a singer completely lost to the gods, and standing that close to the ceiling, I could feel the glory, the adoration of my fans, the clouds of French fry grease. They had paid only a quarter for this performance— almost free. I could track my biggest fan by her hair, the tones of russet and mahogany, sunny apple red, and deep summer wine. I fixated on these colours through the crowd, and they were my anchor. I sang to her, but I also sang to the dead butterfly, the one we had killed somehow. I wanted her to know that the joy and love and good memories we shared were so bright they would fill me with happiness for the rest of my life.

The Du Mauriers gave me a standing ovation.

The Craven A's banged the table with salt shakers and glass ashtrays.

The Export A's stormed out, perhaps suspecting me of betraying their bowling secrets in my interpretive dance.

The Player's wept.

The waitresses waltzed with each other and paid for our meal.

She snapped the photo.

I've had it for years but never studied it. Now I can see someone looking through the window behind me. A man, I think, peering between the jars of bell peppers. The edge of the rounded glass warps his face so I can't see it clearly, but he's smiling, and I can tell he's listening through the window. Beyond his beard, I can see the marshland of his dreads, and beyond the sweat on his massive forehead, I can see the frost setting in. Beyond the summer, I can always see the winter, and beyond the man, there is always the beast.

Now that I think back, we were never not together, not even for a second.

So it's hard to imagine how any of this story could've happened. Outwardly, it's damn near impossible. Yet not all experiences can be explained through a cold retelling of the plausible facts. Sometimes dreams and feelings tell their own particular and peculiar stories, and we must believe them, even when nothing makes sense. There are recurring dreams I haven't told you about yet, persuasive and persistent and violently colourful. Despite the mystery of them, they probably tell me more than memory could. At this point, anyway.

Things turned out differently than how I thought they would. At first, I feared that looking for a bad memory would either upset and shock me or leave me stranded in a dead-end. Instead, it has led me to love and forgiveness, enough to fill any void my memory is capable of creating.

Beyond the song I'm looking for, there's always another more arresting one.

CONTRE LE FROID

I've developed some curious habits of late. They mostly involve the homeless of Montreal.

In winter I seek out the indigent, the people curled around hot air vents in cardboard coffins that don't keep out the cold, wrapped in cocoons of their own devices, functional and unfashionable, screaming their frustration into the piping, the losses and disappointments of long ago and the anguish of the day, wrapped in bacteria and memory, hope filtered through untreated mental illness, beyond depression and into something deeper than polar vortex.

I creep close to hear what they say and how they say it. I catch the fluency and the disfluency. There are many stutterers among the homeless. They have means beyond mine to mangle a language: the growls, mutterings, angry repetitions. Maybe because no one is listening, they are free from expectations, they can finally speak their minds without censorship, and beyond speaking their minds, speak their bodies, allow whatever possesses, ails, and disenfranchises them to come out.

I leave gifts of food in exchange for my eavesdropping. Meals that Eric made. The homeless can keep our best Tupperware.

I suppose I'm just trying to relive my childhood, looking for another Grand Antonio, as if there will ever be another obese prophet of the street, brutish, bravado coasting on the strength of garlic cloves, inventing his own body language for a unique body, reviled and monstrous, worshipped but not rewarded, obscure but convinced of international fame.

What does frost look like as it settles into a cerebral cortex?

It was the coldest night of the year. The firefighters were out fixing burst pipes everywhere. They were too busy with that to deal with the cigarette fires that turned the East End into an inferno. The smoke blew west. Dreams went up in a final puff.

That night, I wanted to hold as many people as possible. I found myself hugging the inconsolable and stinky. Eric kept a lookout while I wrapped my arms and legs around entire torsos. On the coldest night of the year, no one questions your motives, the angles of your limbs. Some of them hugged back. Others gave me a cold shoulder.

I began to notice the shoes of some of the overweight men we visited that night. The soles had given way to their weight, and they split at the sides, letting in all kinds of weather. The men were shocked that we cared, but perhaps more shocked that we gave them plastic bags and elastics instead of new shoes. It felt good to earn the respect of the people who guarded the street, who prevented neighbourhoods from becoming too gentrified and vapid and expensive, who planted tenderness on otherwise faceless corners of urban blight and kept them vital.

Can piss freeze before it's fully pissed out?

It's shocking to lay warm soup at the head of the person who most reminds me of a certain someone, and to cradle their head and shoulders, feel their dandruff fall on me like snowflakes, only to find out much later that they were dead at the time.

It's shocking to cuddle someone under the chassis of a car, anti-freeze leaking onto both of us, feeling the shape they were as a child, and then to realize that a family of cats lives in their coat.

It's shocking to realize how brave the people with the lowest self-esteem are.

There are times when I think that I truly recognize Antonio. When I see a man of no fixed address, hair silvered and long and matted, hundreds of pounds heavier than the nearest curious bystander, verbose and at the top of his sputtering powers, fighting off five police officers, thrashing his way into certain arrest, resist-ing cuffs, and spitting at the law, not intentionally but because the mouth is mysterious with rhythm and fluid, hiding all feelings of resignation behind defiance, he is the only one who doesn't feel sorry for himself, even when they take him down, which they do with nightsticks, frozen over and soon covered in blood. They Taser him and his makeshift shoes rocket off his feet.

You'd think that when the police haul this man away, that it shatters my childhood fantasy. But, in fact, this is when I realize it's Antonio. There has always been an Antonio—there have been many of him—and I can finally let him go. I can collect the shoes as part of forgetting, give them to someone who needs them.

Does snow remember the shape of a body? I get so damn curi-ous in wintertime.

Ultimately we save and help no one.

Usually I was the one who started strange conversations, but this time it was Eric.

I have something to tell you.

Everything has already been said.

Hardly. There are things you don't know about me. Most of which I'll tell you, but some of which I won't.

You need to try a weird kind of sex?

No, I'm not you. First of all, I'll never leave you. It's something I've long known and kept to myself. I want you to hear it from me before you hear it from someone else.

From who?

From *whom*? Nobody.

Well, thanks, that's sweet. But why would you leave me?

I wouldn't.

Then why bring it up? You obviously have more to tell me.

My audiologist said some interesting stuff recently. It looks like I can be treated and there's a good chance it'll...stick.

Huh. Are we talking cochlear implants?

Stapedectomy. I've been saving up, and the bank will finance the rest. I've started to imagine what it's like not being deaf anymore. Weird, eh? And I don't want to feel ashamed for not having any particular attachment to my deafness. What do you think?

Can't say. I don't know your bank.

Not about that, moron.

Um, I don't know what to think. Maybe if you ask me something specific.

Will you ever leave me?

Don't be silly. Of course I'll never leave you. But I want you to think about something. When we start speaking differently to each other, we'll be different people, no? So if one of us left the other, it would be like leaving a new person. Or something like that. We'll probably be drifting in and out of strangerhood for the rest of our lives, anyway. That's what people do.

The threat of taking your deaf jokes away, and you're already acting out. Let's go home.

I can't. I'm busy.

Doing what? It's late.

I'm going for fries with my mom. There's a song she hasn't heard in a long time.

I walked beside Eric as a believer. The future would not always be tainted by the smell of the past, the unheard screams into air vents. We were not Catholic, but we prayed to the icicles on the dome of l'Oratoire Saint-Joseph in the shape of crutches no longer needed, we prayed to the frost on the cross on the mountain, to the snow on the wings of the angel statue, to the muddy slush holes in perpetual construction sites on Boulevard Saint-Laurent. We projected onto precipitation the uncertain construction of our lives because we knew that, at some point, it would melt, and we would be free of it.

AFTERWORD: Lost and in Trouble Somewhere

Sarah Schulman

An open-hearted boy becomes a dog he saw on TV and sloshes through the Montreal snow to catch the next bus. There he meets the mysterious stranger, a man whose touch is like "being bashed by a warm, raw steak."

Reading Daniel's books has always been like reading a well-made movie; there are fade-ins, split screens, and dissolves. With *Mouthquake*, his fourth novel, the movie has become a soundtrack. We now hold something abstract that floats through air, filled with substance, sustenance but not reliant on materiality. You know, like sex and music.

He helps us understand our own experiences by softly bringing detail to life. Thaw matters and marks time. Ice melts to reveal loss. Quebec is seen through the real and imagined lens of icons domestic and imported: Buffy Sainte-Marie as an actual Saint, Craven A's and Export A's, clean-cut baseball becomes bored Expos fans raining garbage on the field. Freddie Mercury, two years before AIDS, declares himself an "anti-monarchist" unless he is the monarch. Marilyn Monroe never actually comes through except in men and women's hearts. Truth interspersed with some facts becomes reality, that thing no one wants to face.

In the tradition of Gail Scott and Jack Kerouac and Robert Glück, Daniel slices open the experience of experience, sometimes with insight, sometimes with threat. The dog becomes a boy who becomes the object of a police interrogation on the subject of his relationship to this man. Who is the predator? The man? The cop? The boy? The publisher of this book? Someone wants something they are not supposed to have. So many questions in the reader's lap. It's scary. Telling the emotional truth means being accused of lying about the facts. Daniel communicates to us through this child "how easily the kind people of the world are destroyed."

Good writers ask important questions of readers, but rarely do they literally write, "How come you don't practice the techniques you learned in therapy?" The priority, of course, is, "How come?" the Why, indifferent to specifics of "technique." Hearing and facing tough questions is so enriching, it makes evolutionary thinking more possible. And through this growth process the reader turns into the writer. The stutterer. And is welcomed to enter his voice.

Mouthquake tells of childhood in Quebec, of a boy in danger. It's a story of the streets, the *stade*, the weather, of what was on the radio, of memory. Of the teenager who listens to the Violent Femmes, has his own band, goes out, becomes a man, moves in with others his own age, drinks Baby Duck red wine, and learns about the "luxury of opulent squalor." Living with his friends, he learns how to take care of himself and others by coming home to each other, talking over their day with each other, and dealing with the art of autonomy, the language of their own responsibility to try, and also to try to figure life out actively. Mutual witnessing is the necessary intimacy of young people leaning through each other, and writers capture this mid-air. Really living is, after all, the greatest inspiration. That's the start of understanding. Becoming an artist is not something you wait to do. Just like becoming a man. Postpone for too long and you never learn how to give, only to take and to waste time, wait, and eventually stop talking big. Being is doing and doing is becoming. That's what stories are all about.

By living with others he becomes a man and finds a boyfriend whom he can recognize is the better lover, "more thoughtful, more responsible, more forgiving." The narrator stutters, Eric is deaf. Sex produces its own imagination, and the knowledge of desire creates more desire. Eric tells him things he doesn't want to face, and yet those things are true and show the narrator to be both seen and loved. People will kill you for seeing them and loving them, for believing they can be what they crave and can have what they can't dare to want beyond a whisper. The narrator is smart enough to let it change him.

Art both tells and transforms life. And it is through the juxtaposition of evocative, surprising language with intellectual awareness and the sharing of open consciousness that this process is conveyed with soul, as long as the form emerges from the emotional center of the work. Daniel finds these connections and innovations within himself, partially through commitment, partially through instinct. It's that thing we call *talent* combined with the hard work of honest feeling, the self-reflection that reveals new selves when a person finally stops defending and decides to understand.

— *New York City, 2015*

ACKNOWLEDGMENTS

Limitless gratitude goes to:

My mother, for a lifetime of love and protection that is the gold standard that I learn from and strive to apply.

Mark Ambrose Harris, for the inspiration of your edifying work and outlook on the world, for believing, for your help with the book, for pushing me forward when the sounds were hard to articulate, for teachings in love and music, for everything. Where would I be without you?

Sarah Schulman, for a body of work that has taught me how to write differently, for your endless justice work, for lending amplification to those who need it, for creating freedom and empowerment and bonds that didn't exist before, for your afterword. Your strength carries me and many others.

The gang at Arsenal Pulp Press: Brian Lam for coaxing shape into my work over the years, and for being a solid champion of texts that others are afraid to publish; Robert Ballantyne for your perception and wisdom; Susan Safyan, my editor, for your exquisite touch. How many times have I sailed off the flat world and into your hands? All books are a collaboration between writer and reader and publisher and editor, even when the editor tries to erase her footsteps; Cynara Geissler, for your genius on how to address a book outside of its pages; Gerilee McBride for a gorgeous design and stunning cover; unseen proofreaders, for your care.

Thomas Waugh, Amber Dawn, John Greyson, and Anakana Schofield, for your jaw-dropping work and the paths it has opened, for your friendship and guidance, for your willingness to inhabit the fringe especially when it's a dangerous place, and for your sweet endorsements.

Francisco Ibáñez-Carrasco, David Rimmer, and Marcus McCann for your brilliance and for helping me hear the sound of my voice.

Natalija Grgorinić and Ognjen Rađen for so warmly welcoming me to the ZVONA i NARI Library & Literary Retreat in Ližnjan, Croatia, and for our ongoing collaborations on either side of the Adriatic blue. How thrilling to experiment with you.

Jordan Coulombe for publishing part of the chapter "Coprofagia," in a different form, in *Crooked Fagazine*, Issue 2. You rock.

David Homel for your jeweller's eye.

Alison Slattery for the portrait and for not letting me evade the lens.

The Grand Antonio for letting your weirdness shine.

The Conseil des arts et des lettres du Québec, whose financial support made the writing of this book possible.

And lastly, to all who bravely interact with sounds that are strange and new, when you don't exactly know what they mean. Sometimes we have to broadcast on unused frequencies to signal to each other the loudest.

You are all a sonic boom.

Love,
DAC

Daniel Allen Cox is the author of the novels *Shuck, Krakow Melt* (both Lambda Literary Award finalists), *Basement of Wolves, Mouthquake,* and the novella *Tattoo This Madness In.* He co-wrote the screenplay for Bruce LaBruce's 2013 film *Gerontophilia.* Daniel is a 2015 writer-in-residence at the ZVONA i NARI Library & Literary Retreat in Ližnjan, Croatia, the first Canadian writer to be invited. He lives in Montreal, where he is vice president of the Quebec Writers' Federation.